May the Best Man Win

Also available in the Road to Avonlea Series

Next in the Series...

May the Best Man Win

Storybook written by

Gail Hamilton

Based on the Sullivan Films Production
written by Grahame Woods
adapted from the novels of

Lucy Maud Montgomery

HarperCollins*Publishers*Ltd

MAY THE BEST MAN WIN
Storybook written by Gail Hamilton

Copyright © 1992 by HarperCollins Publishers Ltd,
Sullivan Films Distribution Inc., and
Ruth Macdonald and David Macdonald

Based on the Sullivan Films Production produced by Sullivan Films Inc.
in association with CBC and the Disney Channel with the participation of
Telefilm Canada adapted from Lucy Maud Montgomery's novels.

Road to Avonlea is the trademark of Sullivan Films Inc.

Teleplay written by Grahame Woods
Copyright © 1990 by Sullivan Films Distribution Inc.

Canadian Cataloguing in Publication Data
Hamilton, Gail
May the best man win
(Road to Avonlea; 17)
Based on the Sullivan Films Production adapted from the novels of
Lucy Maud Montgomery.
ISBN 0-00-647398-9

I. Title. II. Series.

PS8565.A55M39 1992   jC813'.54   C92-094438-8
PZ7.H35Ma 1992

Design by Andrew Smith Graphics Inc.
92 93 94 95 96 ❖ OFF 10 9 8 7 6 5 4 3 2 1

Chapter One

Lighthouse Point offered just about everything a photographer could wish for, including majestic red cliffs, surging ocean waves and even, as the name promised, a lighthouse. Yet the photographer in question, one Jasper Dale, was ignoring all these lavish splendors of humanity and nature in an effort to focus his camera upon a rather skimpy little patch of goldenrod. His companion and fellow journalist, Miss Olivia King, was peering up at the spectacular black rain clouds gathering above their heads. How soon, she wondered, would they open up to drench everything in sight?

"How does it look?" Olivia asked, hoping for a little speed on Jasper's part.

Jasper, at the moment, was nothing but a pair of long, ungainly legs supporting a body almost completely hidden under the camera's black focusing cloth.

"Oh, uh, not bad...not bad at all," came the muffled answer.

The cloth moved and an arm emerged, tilting the camera even further downward. Jasper was a bit of a perfectionist, and he tended to fiddle endlessly in order to get the shot he wanted.

Trying to be patient, Olivia twisted her neck to look skyward again. No sooner had she done so than a tearing clap of thunder made her jump where she stood. Great, fat raindrops came spattering down, striking Olivia's lashes and cheeks and the charming little hat she wore.

"Oh, no! Rain!"

As if to show Olivia what rain really was, the clouds suddenly split, pouring water down by the bucketful. Though it quickly soaked the focusing cloth and Jasper's legs, as well, he was so wrapped up in his work that he didn't even notice. He only began to wonder why the goldenrod had suddenly turned gray.

"It's almost as if the light's gone," he puzzled,

tinkering with the lens and paying no attention to the weather.

By now, Olivia was hopping from foot to foot, trying to protect her hat with her hands and grimacing at her companion.

"Jasper," she finally burst out, "I'm getting soaked!"

At that cry of distress, the rest of Jasper Dale popped out from under the focusing cloth, revealing a long, gangly body to match the lanky legs. The whole was topped with a startled face and tousled, auburn hair mussed by the cloth, and little round spectacles swiftly getting splattered with rain.

"Oh, uh, oh my gosh, it's raining. Uh, no wonder I couldn't get it focused."

Grabbing up the camera and the tripod he began to run, the cloth flapping around his legs and threatening to send him flying at every step. Olivia, in front of him, had begun to run too, but, glancing over her shoulder, she spotted something Jasper had left behind.

"Oh, look, the camera box!"

In spite of Jasper's frantic gestures, she raced back and grabbed it. Since Olivia and Jasper had taken to working together on their assignments for the Avonlea *Chronicle*, Olivia had come to understand a great deal about photography. The camera box, full of the precious photographic plates she and Jasper had worked so hard to get, absolutely could not be left to soak in the rain.

Jasper stopped to wait for her, struggling to keep his balance and much distressed about the great big raindrops now pelting Olivia's back. He would gladly have fended them off with his bare hands, if he'd had a hand to spare, or a chance against the pouring rain.

"Come on, quickly!" he urged, swaying under his load.

When Olivia was almost up to him, Jasper tried to make a grab for the camera box too, knowing a gentleman, however overloaded with wet cameras and tripods, would never let a lady carry such a bulky thing.

"You should...you should...let me..."

Gracefulness, especially while stumbling about in overgrown, soaking grass, was certainly not Jasper's strong point. His efforts to help Olivia nearly sent him, face first, into the goldenrod.

"No, it's all right. I've got it," cried Olivia, applying both hands to the varnished box and speeding up her step. "I've got it."

Jasper lurched after Olivia. The two of them rushed towards the only shelter in sight—a rickety lean-to on the end of an old barn standing at the edge of the farm adjacent to Lighthouse Point. The lean-to was merely a few weathered boards ready to fall down with the next windstorm. It did offer protection from the rain, however, and the two refugees fled gratefully inside.

Jasper managed to put down his load and turn around just as Olivia rushed in. She was so out of breath from sprinting with the camera box, laced up as she was in her tight corsets, that Jasper feared she was going to topple over. Without even thinking what he was doing, Jasper grasped her by the waist from behind to steady her—a liberty he would never have dared take had he stopped for even a fraction of a second to reflect upon his own audacity.

Up until the rain had hit, Jasper Dale and Olivia King had been acting like jolly companions, rambling through the countryside looking for stands of goldenrod and cascades of wild grape vines to photograph for their assignment. But now, under the lean-to, with his hands on Olivia's waist, everything suddenly seemed different to Jasper. He stood still and forgot all about continuing to breathe. His glasses steamed up in front of his eyes and his heart seemed to jump right out of its place inside his chest.

As for Olivia, her heart, too, did a funny little dance that had nothing at all to do with her race through the rain. Then, just when she was thinking how wonderful it felt to be supported by Jasper Dale, Jasper realized how nice Olivia was to hold on to, and he let go of her as though she were a red-hot coal. To cover his embarrassment, he whipped off his spectacles and began cleaning them vigorously with a vast white handkerchief pulled from his coat pocket.

"It's...it's a blur," he mumbled. "Everything's a blur."

No longer hidden behind the spectacles, Jasper's eyes were kind and intelligent, and his features had a manly appeal of their own, when not caught up in the throes of embarrassment or agitation. Still flustered, Jasper suddenly busied himself with his tripod, and almost succeeded in knocking the camera right onto the dirt floor.

Jasper Dale suffered from more than his share of agitation. Despite being a clever photographer and amazingly ingenious at fixing up any sort of contraption, he was one of those people who turned into a bumbling, tongue-tied knot as soon as another human being showed up nearby.

In fact, Jasper Dale had, until recently, been Avonlea's shiest recluse, nicknamed the Awkward Man, until Olivia King, aided and abetted by her niece, Sara Stanley, had winkled him out of his seclusion and persuaded him to apply his talent as a photographer to this job.

Jasper put his spectacles back on and blinked at Olivia through them. What he saw was a cloud of dark hair starred with raindrops, rosy cheeks flushed from the race for shelter, and eyes full of sparkles at the adventure of it all. His heart gave another lurch.

"Perhaps..." he suggested impulsively, "one day you would...pose for me, just a portrait."

One of the reasons Jasper had been a recluse was that he was afflicted with a terrible stutter. In the presence of people with whom he felt comfortable—mainly Olivia King and Sara Stanley—the stutter might almost disappear. When the stutter came back, as it could with a vengeance, it meant either that Jasper was getting agitated, or that his emotions were stirred up.

Right now, his emotions were stirred up. One of the dangers in traipsing about the countryside with Miss Olivia King was that it gave a fellow time to see what pretty hands she had, and how easy she was to talk to, and how merrily she laughed. It started a fellow thinking how wonderful it might be to bask in her company forever.

Olivia, with the warm imprint of Jasper's hands still on her waist, was feeling more than a little strange herself. She, too, had not been unaffected by the photographic journeys. Jasper Dale was about the kindest, cleverest man she had ever met. He had the most endearing way of pulling at his hair when he got upset. And, oh, a great deal of the time, he could be so deliciously funny!

Olivia laughed and looked away.

"Why would you waste a photographic plate on me, Jasper? We want to find news, not make it."

"Oh, no, no, not at all," Jasper sputtered hastily, tangling himself up in his efforts to find a plausible reason. "You are...that's not it at all. You are very...newsworthy."

Perhaps luckily for Jasper, he was saved from having to explain himself by the tramp of heavy hooves and the nicker of a horse. A large, stocky, dour-looking man appeared leading a team of work horses, still in harness. His battered old hat was crammed forward on his head in a direct challenge to the world, and he glowered at the sight of Olivia and Jasper huddled in the lean-to.

"Hey, you two. You're trespassing! You know that, don't you?"

"Well, we were sh-shel—"

"—sheltering from the rain," Olivia finished for Jasper, who was bound to fall into an awful stutter in front of glowering farmers.

The man didn't have the least sympathy for such weak excuses. He met rainstorms head on and thought that anyone else with any gumption should do so too.

"Well, it's stopped, so be off," he barked rudely, appearing not to have a hospitable impulse in him.

Indeed, it wasn't raining any more—a fact neither Olivia nor Jasper had got round to noticing yet.

Their host was about to tramp off with his team when he spotted the camera and tripod lying under the black cloth at Jasper's feet and approached, a suspicious look in his eye.

"What're you doing here, anyway?" he demanded, his tone clearly accusing the two of being up to no good.

Jasper, taking exception, whipped back the black cloth proudly.

"As you can see, this is photographic equipment."

"I'm writing an article for the Avonlea *Chronicle*," Olivia added importantly, "on autumn flora and fauna in—"

"No—no photographs," the man growled. "It's bad luck! Now get off my property."

Something in the man's expression said he had already had too much bad luck in his life. Wanting no trouble, Jasper and Olivia hastily gathered up their gear and headed back towards Jasper's buggy, which was parked under a tree nearby.

As they hurried back across the wet grass, they were completely unaware of another observer. As the man with the team moved off, a wide-eyed boy of about eight slipped from behind a broad tree trunk, where he had been hiding and watching the exchange by the lean-to. He was so curious about Olivia and Jasper that he eventually followed them, accompanied by his enormous black Newfoundland dog, to Jasper's buggy and watched, unnoticed, as they packed the equipment into the back. Finally, he edged around the tailgate and stood beside the wheel.

"Oh, Jasper," Olivia was saying, pausing to brush water from Jasper's damp lapels. She was smiling indulgently at Jasper's soggy, bedraggled outfit when a completely unexpected little voice piped up just behind her.

"Hello!" the boy said cheerily.

Olivia's hand fell away from Jasper's coat and they both turned around in surprise.

"Oh, hello," returned Olivia, smiling even wider at the cloth cap perched askew and the jam smears ornamenting the little fellow's cheeks. The jam overlaid smudges of dirt, while rips in the front of the boy's overalls showed that no one in his house had felt like doing any mending recently.

The dog, determined not to be left out, insinuated itself between the boy and Olivia's skirt. Its great pink tongue lolled out in a doggy smile as it seemed to demand an introduction, too.

"Well, who belongs to whom?" Olivia asked, bending down to pat the friendly monster.

"That's Rufus," the boy informed her. "I'm Teddy Armstrong. You were talking to my dad, weren't you?"

"Ch-ch-charming fellow," Jasper commented tartly.

"I'm Olivia King and this is Jasper Dale," Olivia told Teddy politely in return.

Deciding that Teddy was as harmless as his dad was sour, Jasper, too, bent down. He really did like children, provided they were not of the nasty, teasing sort.

"How do you do?" he said, solemnly shaking the boy's hand.

Teddy had only one hand free to take care of social amenities. The other was busy clutching half of a fat jam turnover.

"He's really very nice, my dad," Teddy insisted, anxious that Jasper and Olivia not think badly of the man. "He's just feelin' a little bad ever since Ma died."

Teddy took another bite of the turnover, then held it out to Olivia.

"Would you like a bite? My dad made it."

Evidently, Jim Armstrong did not deny his son a few treats, which added considerably to his merits in Olivia's eyes.

"I'd love one," she replied, knowing how rude it would be to turn down Teddy's offer. "I'm sorry about your mum. Hetty told me that you left school about six months ago."

Hetty King was Olivia's older sister and also the Avonlea schoolteacher. Naturally, Hetty was concerned when a pupil as young as Teddy disappeared from the classroom.

Teddy nodded mournfully. "My dad won't let me go. He reads a lot of books himself, and he says he's gonna teach me. But right now he don't have much time, runnin' our farm and workin' for Jeb Sloan, too."

At that moment, Teddy presented such a picture of wistfulness, curiosity, jam-smeared charm and desire to please that Olivia suddenly whirled towards Jasper.

"Jasper, we should take a—"

"—photograph," Jasper finished for her, already setting up the tripod again.

Olivia laughed aloud, more than a little unnerved

by how swiftly Jasper had read her thoughts. "I guess we think alike," she said.

As Jasper adjusted the camera, Olivia produced a handkerchief, meaning to wipe the jam from Teddy's face. Instantly, Jasper laid his hand on her shoulder.

"No! Stop! Just leave it. See, that's the photograph, that's...that's Teddy."

When Jasper was doing what he loved to do, he could move with surprising speed and decision. Now, caught up in the throes of artistic inspiration, Jasper flung the black cloth over himself and pressed his eye to the camera underneath.

"Let's have a smile," he instructed Teddy, waving one hand like an orchestra leader from under the cloth. Teddy obliged with the sort of huge, enchanting grin only a jammy eight-year-old can manage.

Olivia held up the flash, entranced with Teddy, too. The flash went off with a great *whoosh* and Teddy Armstrong was immortalized forever on one of Jasper's plates.

Chapter Two

Rose Cottage was a pretty house not far from the village of Avonlea, with wide verandas and lots of white-painted scrollwork ornamenting the gables. Olivia King lived there along with her sister, Hetty, and their niece, the lively, imaginative Sara Stanley.

Inside, Olivia had just trotted downstairs to the hall mirror to check that her hat pin was in securely. With a glance towards the front door, she stepped into the kitchen, where Hetty was putting up plum preserves.

"I can't stay, Hetty," Olivia chirped, far too cheerfully for Hetty's taste. "Jasper's coming to pick me up in a few minutes."

Olivia was the youngest of the grown-up Kings, and Hetty—being the eldest and considerably older than Olivia—regarded herself as the watchdog over Olivia's activities and the general overseer of Olivia's life. She was not the least bit happy about Olivia's airy announcement, and she showed it by drawing her mouth into a prune.

"It strikes me as being somewhat unseemly, Olivia, you spending so much time in the company of Jasper Dale, of all people."

While Olivia still retained the lively freshness of youth, Hetty was angular, middle-aged and more than a little fixed in her ideas about propriety. And, of course, since Hetty had never succumbed to the flatteries of a gentleman and was therefore not married, she regarded herself as an infallible authority on proper behavior with men.

In contrast to Hetty, Olivia was meek and pliable by nature, always trying to keep the peace and normally giving way to Hetty's wishes. It was quite unusual for Olivia to get annoyed, so Hetty was more than a little surprised by the answer she got to her remark.

"Hetty, our relationship is strictly professional," Olivia shot back. "He's the only photographer in Avonlea; he takes very good photographs. They complement my text."

Hetty, dressed in a work smock, her hair scraped back into a bun, ladled more yellow plums into one of the dozen jars iined up on the table in front of her and gave a loud sniff.

"That's about all he'd complement. Oh, I have no patience with his bumbling, awkward manners, his, his... Really, the man's exasperating beyond words."

Hetty herself was a woman of action and discipline, constitutionally unable to abide anyone who dithered in her presence. So, naturally, Jasper Dale began to dither at the mere mention of Hetty's name.

Before the argument could progress further, Sara Stanley dashed down the stairs and headed for the front door. She'd almost made her escape when Hetty spotted her.

"Sara!"

A second member of the household seemed bent on insubordination. Putting down her ladle, Hetty marched into the front hall, intent upon intercepting the culprit.

"And where do you think you're going?"

"I'm going to help Felicity decorate the King barn for the church social," Sara said virtuously. "She's expecting me."

Wise in the ways of her aunt, Sara then sped out the door before Hetty could commandeer her for an afternoon of scalding plums over a red-hot stove. How much more delightful to be working on the barn with her cousin, Felicity King! Felicity would supply the materials and Sara the inspiration. Between them, the barn ought to look absolutely glorious for the church social.

As Sara ran down the steps of Rose Cottage, Jasper Dale was just pulling up in his buggy.

"Hello, Mr. Dale," Sara called out, not daring to stop while still within range of Hetty's voice.

"Oh, hello, S-Sara! Oh, and g-goodbye."

Jasper watched, bemused, as Sara galloped off through the gate and out of sight. Sara was one of Jasper's special friends in Avonlea, and he was used to enjoying a bit of a chat with her whenever they met. Why, if Sara Stanley hadn't prodded him into giving a magic lantern show in the Avonlea Town Hall that time, he might still be hiding out up in his photographic studio. He'd still be avoiding people on the street and would never have dared even pass the time of day with Miss Olivia King. Yes, lucky for him, Sara Stanley had a talent for making friends with the most unusual people.

Hetty glowered through the window at Jasper Dale's arrival.

"There he is. A shiftless milquetoast is all, steeped in the foul stench of photographic chemicals!"

When Hetty took a dislike to someone, as she had to Jasper, she hadn't a scrap of subtlety in her. She always chose a direct attack—which was exactly the wrong way to dampen Olivia's growing enthusiasm for her friend. Olivia's brows flew together fiercely as she pulled open the front door.

"Hetty King," she snapped, "it would behoove you to be more *Christian* towards your neighbors!"

At this severe reproach from mild Olivia, Hetty's hand flew up to her face in genuine shock. She began to suspect that the situation with Jasper Dale was far more serious than even she had imagined.

"Oh, my, my," she said dramatically. "Me thinks she doth—"

The door slammed behind Olivia, making the vase on the side table jump in its place.

"—protest too much!"

Olivia stormed down the porch steps and up into Jasper's buggy, sitting down hard enough to make the buggy rock on its springs. Jasper, who had rarely seen anything but smiles on Olivia's face, reared back in some alarm.

"Are you all right?" he asked diffidently.

Olivia released a heated breath. "Just a slight attack of 'Hetty Kingitis'. She loves to put a damper on my friendships."

Knowing just who Hetty was trying to put a damper on, Jasper nodded in resignation and tried to look sage.

"Sisters are like that. I'm led to believe they can, you know, love and hate each other at the same time."

This was fine for Jasper to say. He had had no personal experience with sisters of his own. Olivia jerked her head vehemently.

"She'd be happy if I were a complete recluse with no social contact whatsoever."

Since Olivia made not the faintest attempt to muffle her words, they carried up the steps and straight into Rose Cottage, where Hetty still stood by the door, overhearing every one.

"I just wish she would stop meddling in my life," Olivia finished furiously as Jasper picked up the reins and they drove off.

Hetty was left peering after them through the lace curtains, her eyes snapping and her heart thumping with alarm. Oh, how horrible to suspect that Olivia might actually be hatching an infatuation for the "shiftless milquetoast"! And how equally horrible to feel helpless to do anything about it.

After a moment, though, Hetty straightened her back and set her lips more firmly together. Deep down, Hetty didn't believe in helplessness. Needing some time to think, she marched back into the kitchen to take out her ire on the plums.

Sara ran all the way over to the nearby King farm, where the big, peak-roofed barn was waiting to be decorated.

A city girl herself, Sara was totally entranced with the very idea of a party in a barn. What a terrific place, she thought, to cram a lot of people in, have purple punch and dancing, and never give a single thought to anyone scratching up the furniture. Willingly, she helped her cousin, Felix King,

lug boxes of plates and punch glasses out to the
barn while Felix's mother, Janet, stood in her
apron, calculating where to put the refreshment
tables. Felix, at eleven, had never been a big fan of
hard work, even in the cause of entertainment. He
plunked his burden down at his mother's feet and
uttered an aggrieved sigh.

"Mother, how do the Kings get roped into host-
ing all these parties?" he complained.

His mother merely laughed at him, knowing
that, in a few hours, Felix would be joyfully stuffing himself with chocolate cake and nimbly dodg-
ing the dancers as he ran about with his friends.

"Be quiet, Felix," said Sara. "You love it as
much as we do!"

Before Felix could be sent off for another load,
the sound of a buggy approaching made all three
turn to look. It was Olivia and Jasper rattling merrily along the road that led past the King farm.
Jasper was clutching the reins and bracing himself
against the dashboard. Olivia, her fit of temper with
Hetty quite forgotten, was holding onto her hat and
laughing delightedly at Jasper's dashing speed.
When she spotted her relatives grouped in front of
the barn, she gave them all a cheerful wave.

"Hello!" she called out as the buggy sped past,
tossing up gravel from its wheels.

Janet and the two children waved back. Sara was delighted to see the obvious growing attraction between Jasper and her Aunt Olivia. Jasper's sterling qualities were not evident to everyone, however. Janet King put one hand on her hip and tilted her head in bewilderment.

"I wonder what Olivia sees in Jasper Dale," she said in a bemused voice as the pair disappeared behind a stand of young ash trees.

Sara, who probably knew Jasper Dale better than anyone in Avonlea, including Olivia, smiled knowingly.

"He's a gentleman," she returned, "in the true meaning of the word."

Janet was not terribly impressed by such refined qualities. She liked a little boldness, a little fire in a man.

"I think it would be nice if Aunt Olivia were courted by someone with a bit more bounce. That Jasper Dale is doomed to bachelorhood, I'm sure."

"Well, if you want my opinion—" Felix began.

"We don't," declared Sara, cutting her cousin off firmly as she went on into the barn.

"Aunt Olivia and Jasper are far too ancient to get married," Felix continued, turning to his mother. "They're almost as old as you and Father!"

Felix then followed Sara through the open barn door, leaving his mother with her mouth open in exasperation. She might be the mother of three, but she certainly wasn't ready to be called ancient—especially by an opinionated eleven-year-old boy!

Chapter Three

If there was anything the people of Avonlea loved, it was a good party. By late afternoon, buggies were streaming down the road, the lilting music was drifting through the hayloft, and a horde of thirsty dancers was putting away vast quantities of Janet King's excellent fruit punch.

Hetty and Sara, dressed up for the occasion and each carrying a covered dish with their contribution of food, opened the side door and stepped into all the music and jollity. Hetty gazed about in admiration as she made her way over to a table to set down her offering.

"My, you children have done a fine job, Sara," Hetty told her niece as they edged through the crowd. "Why, I've never seen this barn look quite so festive."

Sara and her cousins had, indeed, outdone themselves in decorating the barn. Its cavernous interior was festive with strings of bright flags running from beam to beam and many bunches of multicolored autumn flowers, artfully arranged in china wash jugs.

"Avonlea has been buzzing about this church social all week," Sara said excitedly, following at her aunt's heels. "I hear that people from Markdale and guests from the White Sands Hotel are expected to attend."

"Oh, my!" exclaimed Hetty, impressed. The nearby White Sands Hotel was an elegant establishment to which wealthy people from all over the country came "to take the air." That the guests of the hotel would condescend to attend a local entertainment was a coup, indeed!

Hetty and Sara stood behind a jug of autumn leaves, watching the dancers go through the steps of a reel. Across the barn, a group of Avonlea ladies gathered with their heads together, the way they did when one of them had an especially juicy morsel of news.

"As I live and breathe," warbled Mrs. Spencer, shaking every flower on her hat, "I heard he's coming tonight, just for old times' sake."

"Who?" Mrs. Lawson wanted to know. Mrs. Lawson ran the Avonlea store, but she tended to be a little slow at picking up on hints.

"Of course," Mrs. Spencer rattled on, "at first, I wasn't sure. He looks somewhat older—"

"Ha! Don't we all," put in Mrs. Inglis with a twitch of her double chin.

"—but Bessie Middleton saw the registration card at the White Sands Hotel this afternoon."

"Who?" Mrs. Biggins demanded, growing positively breathless from suspense.

"Edwin Clark!" crowed Mrs. Spencer triumphantly.

The name rang out over the general din—and froze Hetty King where she stood. She was caught with a piece of plum cake halfway to her lips and a look of very uncomfortable shock on her face.

"*The* Edwin Clark?" Mrs. Inglis asked, her eyes quite round.

"The very one!"

Mrs. Spencer was delighted with the effect upon her audience. Mrs. Lawson frowned, trying to place the name.

"The Edwin Clark who—"

"—ran away with Althea Gillis after Hetty King broke things up between Olivia and him," Mrs. Inglis finished, rushing in to cap the delicious tale.

"And set poor Olivia on a direct road to spinsterhood!" Mrs. Spencer sighed, rolling her eyes to the ceiling.

Sara, who had been looking over the butter tarts, hadn't been listening to the conversation going on a few yards away. This last speech, however, finally caught her attention. Her head snapped up and she stared, unbelieving, at her aunt. Just as all the women giggled and Sara's mouth opened with the inevitable question, Hetty became aware of the effect the conversation was having on her niece. Knowing Sara had enough curiosity for five ordinary children, she came to life and made shooing motions with her hands.

"Go ahead and fetch me some apple cider, will you, dear? Run along, now."

Much as Sara hated to leave, she knew better than to start arguing with her Aunt Hetty. With a couple of backward glances to make sure her aunt wasn't looking, she edged around to the other side of the group of women and hovered there, all the better to overhear more.

"To think, that was all of ten years ago," Mrs. Inglis mused, taking another nibble at the piece of shortbread in her hand.

Mrs. Spencer nodded energetically, not yet finished with her tantalizing fund of news.

"At least. And not only is Edwin Clark back in Avonlea, but he is a widower—God rest Althea's soul—and a very wealthy widower, to boot!"

Edwin Clark wealthy! And a widower! It was a good thing Sara was on the other side of the group, unable to see her Aunt Hetty's eyes widen even further as a whole army of conflicting emotions invaded her face.

"That'll knock Hetty down a peg," cried Mrs. Biggins, who had often been knocked down several pegs herself by Hetty's sharp tongue.

The women all laughed uproariously, which threw Hetty into a near panic. Any moment, one of the women was liable to look around and notice her. Looking about in search of a plausible retreat, Hetty spotted Olivia just coming in the door. Hetty dived towards her sister.

"Oh, Olivia King, where have you been?"

Olivia let out a happy sigh. Her cheeks were suspiciously pink, her eyes a bit misty and her hair plucked into charming tendrils by some thoroughly wanton breeze.

"Oh, it was such a beautiful evening we stopped to listen to the frogs."

"Frogs?" Hetty croaked incredulously, doing a fair imitation of a green amphibian herself.

Then Jasper Dale stepped into the barn behind Olivia, and Hetty realized just who Olivia had been listening to the frogs with. Jasper had honored the occasion by donning his best suit, complete with unevenly buttoned vest and necktie knotted to noose-like tightness. Flustered at Jasper's sudden appearance and unwilling to be civil to the man, Hetty scanned the crowd for her niece.

"Oh, I...I wonder where Sara Stanley is. She's gone to fetch me some apple cider, you see."

A lady in need of refreshment was a call no gentleman could ignore. Besides, Jasper wanted to get away from Hetty as badly as Hetty wanted to get away from him, and the cider provided a dandy excuse. Seizing the opportunity, Jasper turned to Olivia.

"A good idea...uh, Miss King? Some...?"

"Thank you," Olivia answered quickly, before Jasper's tongue became completely tied up.

Having committed himself to the mission, Jasper could then see no way to set out upon it except to step between the two women. With his hat clutched to his chest, he squeezed awkwardly past Hetty, nearly sending her stumbling as he did so. It was only then that he remembered that he ought to have extended his offer to all ladies present.

"Oh, uh, would you like some cider, Miss King? Oh, no, I forgot. S-S-S-"

"Cider?" Hetty supplied, exasperated, trying to guess what word Jasper was fumbling for.

"S-Sara, uh, I forgot..."

As Jasper plunged into the crowd towards the cider keg, Hetty watched him go with a scowl.

"Really, there's not a brain in that man's head. But then, what can you expect from cold soup warmed over?"

Once again, heavy-handed tactics got nowhere with Olivia. Her radiant smile faded in an instant.

"Hetty!" she exploded angrily, and she set out after Jasper.

"No, no, Olivia," Hetty tried to say, but it was absolutely of no use. Olivia was bent on keeping company with the man, and she went so far as to openly grasp his arm.

"Jasper, let's dance!" Olivia cried, determined to show Hetty exactly what she thought of her rude comments.

After years of living as a recluse, it was an enormous testament to Jasper's esteem for Olivia that he was at this social at all. A year ago, wild elephants couldn't have dragged him out to face a crowd like this. But now, to be expected to actually dance as well...!

"Oh!" he cried in dismay as Olivia dragged him towards the open floor.

"Come on!" she laughed, her eyes bright with mirth and determination. Jasper found himself flung, practically head first, into a reel.

In former days, he would simply have stumbled out again and bolted barn, party and everything—back to the refuge of his house. All that had changed, though, since meeting Olivia. Though his feet tried at once to trip over themselves, Jasper stayed with the circle. If Olivia wanted him to dance, then dance he would, even if he expired in the attempt.

The dancers grabbed him, one after the other, and propelled him on in spite of himself. When Jasper found himself, some moments later, still on his feet and actually twirling Olivia round in his arms, his heart swelled ecstatically within him. Why, with such a reward, he could live through a year of waltzes and reels, if only Olivia King swept through them by his side.

At the other end of the barn, the side door near the food table creaked open and a young face popped in. It was Teddy Armstrong, irresistibly drawn by the music and all the fun going on inside. His eyes lit up just from all the colorful sights around him. Then he spied Felix loading up his plate from the lavish spread of desserts.

"Felix!" Teddy whispered. Then, seeing that Felix was totally absorbed in making choices, he whispered still louder, "Felix!"

Felix half turned and burst into a grin.

"Teddy!"

Vigorously, Felix waved Teddy over to the pastry table, where their eyes gleamed with all the fabulous delights.

"My dad would skin me alive if he knew I was here," Teddy confessed, then added wistfully, "I'm supposed to be home finishing chores, but I was hopin' I'd see all you fellas here."

Because Teddy hadn't been to school for six months, it was only natural that he missed all his friends terribly—so terribly that he had sneaked across the lonely fields to the forbidden social to see them. And sneaking across fields was hungry work! Felix saw the direction of Teddy's gaze and immediately shoved his loaded plate towards his friend.

"Oh, here, have some."

"Thanks!"

Teddy clutched his bounty, waiting while Felix heaped desserts on another plate for himself. Then the two boys slipped outside, where Teddy's dog, Rufus, was eagerly waiting. Sara followed them out.

"Do you intend to *eat* all that?" she demanded, pointing to the load of food they were carrying.

"We're gonna try," Felix and Teddy echoed in happy unison.

Felix rose to the occasion by introducing his friend. "Sara, you remember Teddy Armstrong, don't you?"

"How are you, Teddy?" Sara smiled and gave Rufus a pat. Rufus had his eye on the pastries, but was restraining himself until invited. Restraint was a very necessary quality in a dog as large as the Newfoundland.

"He's a friendly thing, isn't he?" Sara said.

"He sure likes people!" exclaimed Teddy with such force that anyone might think it was himself he was talking about. And probably Rufus didn't like sitting around a lonesome farm with a grief-stricken man any more than Teddy did.

"When are you coming back to school, Teddy?" Sara wanted to know. She tended to share her aunt's views on education.

Teddy let out a tremendous sigh. "Never. My dad says it's run by a bunch of hypocrites, and, besides, he wants me to work on the farm." It never occurred to Teddy that Sara's Aunt Hetty was the "hypocrite" his father had meant.

Sara didn't have a chance to reply because the attention of all of the children was distracted by the arrival of a spanking new buggy driven by a man turned out in an immaculate top hat and fashionable topcoat that twirled from his shoulders like a cloak.

"Who's that?" Felix asked, stuffing his mouth with a luscious butter tart.

"Probably another guest from the White Sands." Sara was more interested in Teddy and Rufus than the handsome stranger with the bold manner, who was probably just a hotel guest come to look in at the local party.

The man got down from the buggy, then looked irritably at the horse. Horses could not simply be left standing for hours hitched up to buggies while their drivers enjoyed themselves at parties. Horses had to be made comfortable too—and the man, at that moment, apparently did not feel like doing it. He looked around and spotted the children. Cheap child labor immediately popped into his mind.

"Hey, you boys there," he rapped out arrogantly, "give me a hand with this buggy. I don't want my horse hitched up all night. I'll tell you what. If you brush him down and walk him around the yard, I'll give you a nickel."

A whole nickel! Teddy jumped up as though his legs were springs, his eyes eager. Used to all sorts of hard work for no money at all, a nickel seemed an enormous sum.

"I'll do it, sir. I'll walk him."

With a grin that would have seemed altogether

too sly to a more knowing observer, the man left Teddy to the job and headed for the festivities in the barn.

Chapter Four

The new arrival opened the barn door and stepped inside, immediately running into the very knot of Avonlea ladies who had been gossiping happily a short time before. All of them stared far more than was polite, and gave delighted gasps.

"Oh, my!" whispered Mrs. Lawson. "Edwin Clark!"

So, this swaggering stranger was none other than the much-discussed Edwin, now wealthy, now widowed and now returned to Avonlea an eligible man.

Indeed, Edwin Clark entering the church social might just as well have been Prince Charming returning in triumph after ten years of conquest in the Kingdom of Commerce. The women surrounded him excitedly, not missing the excellent quality of the wool in his coat or the ruddy, well-fed smoothness of his face.

"Why Mrs. Lawson," Edwin exclaimed, shaking her hand and deliberately turning on the charm.

Mrs. Biggins rushed up. "How nice to see you, Mr. Clark," she burbled, insisting that her hand be shaken, too. Mrs. Biggins kept the boarding house in Avonlea and was immensely impressed by anyone with the wherewithal to stay at the grand White Sands Hotel.

"Delighted to see you again, Mrs. Biggins," Edwin said, proving his excellent memory.

"Welcome back to Avonlea," Mrs. Lawson offered, as preamble to what was to be an even more hospitable speech.

To tell the truth, Edwin wasn't the least bit interested in Mrs. Lawson or Mrs. Biggins. Before the storekeeper could continue, Edwin peered past her shoulder and spotted Hetty King. A decidedly mischievous look passed across his face.

"Thank you. Will you excuse me, ladies?" he said to his admirers, abandoning them without a backward glance.

Considering that Hetty had once broken up a romance between Edwin and Olivia, one might assume that Edwin had a bone to pick with the head of the King family. As he took care to approach her from behind, he did look as though he were stalking her, and only at the very last moment did he step around to confront her head on.

"Good evening, Miss King," he drawled, removing his hat with a flourish. *Look how rich and grand I am*, his gesture said. *Aren't you sorry you drove away a catch like me those many years ago?*

If Edwin had thought to take Hetty King aback, he certainly failed. Warned by the gossip she had overheard, Hetty had been expecting him. And, what's more, she had spent the interval thinking hard about all Edwin's money and his eligible status, even as she glowered at Olivia cavorting about the dance floor with Jasper Dale. Swallowing down her initial shock, Hetty actually managed a welcoming smile for the visitor.

"Mr. Clark. Nice to see a successful son of Avonlea return to the Island. What brings you home?"

"I've sold my mother's property," Edwin told her, taken a little off balance by this warm welcome. "I'm just tidying up some of her affairs. I thought I'd stop by and see some old friends."

Hetty had a pretty shrewd idea of just which "old friend" he had come to see, and this time, she intended to be just as helpful as she could. She pointed straight across the floor to the whirling dancers.

"I'm sure Olivia, for one, will be delighted to see you. She's never, ah, given her hand to anyone, you know." Then, as if this invitation wasn't clear enough, Hetty came right out and said, "She's not married."

If this wasn't unconditional approval of Edwin and a signal to get into action, Edwin didn't know what was. Slightly amazed at this about-face, Edwin paused while a dozen little wheels spun round in his head. His own high opinion of himself grew even higher. He broke into a grin as he saw Olivia weaving in and out.

"Glad to hear it. You'll excuse me, Miss King?"

Edwin made his way to the edge of the dancers and stood watching Olivia. He saw that she was still young, still pretty, and that she could still laugh in the most enchanting manner, as her laughter with Jasper Dale at that very moment amply demonstrated. Giving Jasper no more than a glance, Edwin suddenly decided to join the dance. He grabbed one of the men stepping past and expertly extracted the fellow from the reel, inserting himself in his place.

"Excuse me," he said to the astonished dancer, and went tripping on his way.

"Who's that?" asked Sara, coming over to join her Aunt Hetty. Sara had noticed how intently Hetty was staring at the new arrival and had her own strong suspicions about the man's identity.

What's more, Sara had been around Rose Cottage long enough to recognize when her Aunt Hetty was hatching a scheme.

Sara's voice startled Hetty out of her satisfied reverie. Through previous uncomfortable experience, Hetty had learned that Sara was an exceedingly perceptive child, and, at the moment, Hetty didn't feel like being seen through.

"Never you mind, child," Hetty crackled out. Then she added, "Just you promise me, Sara, when your turn comes around, you won't get all bamboozled by this love business. Lord knows love will wither on the vine if a man has no prospects at all."

Olivia and Jasper were dancing a Scottish reel, with several young men in kilts flying past them. Jasper, though getting into the spirit, was still pretty haphazard about ending up where he was supposed to be. Preoccupied with keeping his balance as the other ladies swung him round, he was at the far end of the circle from Olivia when she whirled round beside a pillar—and found herself face to face with Edwin Clark. Speechless, Olivia and Edwin came to a complete halt, letting the other dancers rollick on without them.

"Edwin Clark," Olivia gasped, as though a ghost of past romance had suddenly risen up before her from the floor.

"I didn't expect it to happen quite this way, Olivia," he crooned, hovering over her. "But I *was* hoping to run into you."

Over by the wall, like a soppy Greek chorus, Mrs. Spencer, Mrs. Inglis, Mrs. Lawson and Mrs. Biggins all craned their necks in fascination. It was almost more of a thrill than they could bear, seeing two cruelly parted lovers meeting again, many years later, before their very eyes.

"Why doesn't he *do* something?" Mrs. Lawson urged, fluttering her lashes.

"Like what?" asked Mrs. Inglis, who was lamentably short of imagination.

Mrs. Lawson's bosom heaved ardently. "I don't know. Kiss her or something?"

They each sighed at the poetry of it all, even as they saw Edwin draw Olivia deftly aside.

On the other side of the reel, Jasper found himself abruptly without a partner. The sight of Olivia, standing stock-still and gazing up into the face of the handsome Edwin, almost sent Jasper flying into a mound of hay. He stumbled out of the reel and stood clumsily to one side. The same tender tableau that had inspired fond sentiments in the hearts of the Avonlea ladies struck dismay in the heart of Jasper Dale.

"Forgive me for being so forward," Edwin was

saying, not in the least contrite for having rudely elbowed his way in front of Olivia in the dance, "but you are as beautiful as I remember. I'd like to see you again, if I may."

"Oh...!" Olivia was startled, unable to think straight and still not sure that this Edwin Clark standing before her was quite real.

"May I?" Edwin begged, striking a suitably pleading pose.

"No!" came the involuntary squeak from Olivia's throat, throwing Edwin off his stride.

"Wha...?"

"I mean, yes, or...I don't know." Olivia was more confused than ever, and unable to think of a single reason to refuse. "Well...when?"

"How about tomorrow afternoon?"

"Fine," Olivia agreed shakily. "I'll see you then. Excuse me."

Olivia fled to Hetty for cover. Hetty had been watching the scene with open satisfaction. Here, surely, was the end of Jasper Dale.

"The Lord works in mysterious ways, Olivia. I know now I was wrong ten years ago," she said, positively awash in virtue. "I am prepared to admit I should never have pushed away Edwin Clark. No, he's a good man...very successful. So stop acting like an addle-brained schoolgirl."

Hetty seemed unable to be tactful. Olivia came out of her pleased fluster about Edwin to frown at her sister.

"Oh, Hetty—"

Hetty raised her hands in mock humility. "No, I am not going to try to control your life any more, Olivia. My sole concern now is that you find...happiness...with the right person, of course. And the right person certainly isn't Jasper Dale."

Having accomplished his mission with Olivia and swept the rest of Avonlea off their feet besides, Edwin had no interest in staying for the remainder of the social. Shrugging on his expensive topcoat, he stepped out into the dusk.

Seeing him, young Teddy Armstrong struggled to back Edwin's horse into the shafts of the buggy and hitch it up again. Teddy hadn't expected Edwin out for ages, and he'd been eating his pastries with Felix.

"Aren't you ready yet, boy?" Edwin snapped, annoyed, as Teddy fumbled at the traces. Money had made Edwin used to instant service.

"Sorry, sir. Felix and me would'a had him all hitched up if we knew you'd be leavin' so soon. May I have our nickel now?"

Edwin climbed up into the buggy and picked

up the reins as Teddy finished his job. He raised his eyebrows derisively at the expectant lad waiting by the buggy wheel.

"Nickel? I never promised you anything of the kind."

"Yes, you did, sir," Teddy informed Edwin guilelessly. "That's why I walked him and brushed him good."

Boyish innocence and deserving work didn't have the least effect upon Edwin.

"Don't try to hoodwink me. Now, out of the way."

Teddy looked doubly distressed, seeing his hard-earned wage slipping away.

"But, sir, you promised!"

Laughing at such foolish trust, Edwin merely clucked to the horse and drove on his way, nearly running over Teddy in the process.

Chapter Five

It only took a couple of short words from an old flame to set events in Olivia King's life moving at a dizzying speed. The very next morning, a delivery boy was seen by the whole neighborhood pedaling his bicycle up to Rose Cottage and knocking at the door. He was practically hidden by the long white box he was holding in his arms.

"Just a minute," Hetty called out, hurrying from the parlor and wondering who on earth could be at their door so early in the day.

"Flowers for Miss King," the boy announced as the front door swung open.

Astonished, Hetty took the box into her arms and was immediately enveloped in a cloud of exotic fragrances.

"Oh, my, thank you. Thank you very much."

Glad to be rid of so much fanciness, the boy touched his cap and pedaled off again.

Hetty closed the front door, agog with curiosity. When Olivia hurried down the stairs, she found Hetty examining the enclosed card.

"Who on earth sent those?" Olivia exclaimed, staring at the sprays of roses and carnations peeping out from under the tissue paper Hetty had pulled back.

"They're for you," Hetty told her, still admiring the card.

Olivia, who loved pretty things, was both delighted and puzzled.

"They're wonderful...but why would Jasper have gone to so much trouble?"

Jasper Dale indeed! thought Hetty. As if *he* would have the wit to think of flowers!

"From your sincere admirer with warmest

regards, Edwin," Hetty read. Triumphantly, she passed the card to her sister.

Olivia read the card for herself, twice over, and was much moved. The perfume from the blossoms was already drifting through the front hall, and the tissue paper whispered excitingly of much more to come.

"Oh, Hetty, no one's ever sent me flowers like these in my life! And all the way from Charlottetown! Can you imagine!"

Things were going much better than Hetty could have hoped. On the well-tried principle that one must strike while the iron is hot, Hetty sprang into action herself.

"Must have cost a pretty penny, too, I wouldn't doubt. I'll write your thank-you note immediately. Then, uh, Peter can run it over to the White Sands Hotel. Yes. Best we reply to Mr. Edwin Clark *tout de suite!*"

"Sara, come and see the flowers!" Olivia called up the stairs. "I'd better put them in water right away."

Sara did come down the stairs, but she came very slowly, and she looked very dubious. Sara had her heart set on a romance—a romance, that is, between her Aunt Olivia and her dear friend, Jasper Dale. At the social, she had taken an instant

dislike to Edwin Clark. She hadn't missed the way
he had commandeered her Aunt Olivia from the
dance, and she certainly wasn't pleased about the
arrival of flowers from him now.

Yet even before Sara got to the bottom of the
stairs, her worries were increased. She couldn't
help overhearing her Aunt Hetty in the front
room, where she had settled at her desk.

"Clara Potts tells me that Edwin Clark has
decided to extend his stay in Avonlea," Hetty was
saying, with obvious satisfaction in her voice, as
she composed the thank-you note.

Olivia carried her booty into the kitchen, where
she found a vase, filled it with water and started
arranging the flowers artistically. Sara followed
her in and stood gloomily beside the kitchen table.

"He wants to see me this afternoon," Olivia con-
fided, flushed at the prospect and, truth to tell, more
than a little carried away by the extravagant gift.
"Perhaps he's still fond of me after all these years.
After all, his wife is gone.... God rest her soul."

Naturally, it was very exciting to be suddenly
courted anew by a former suitor, one who she
thought had vanished forever. Feeling that Olivia
was in danger of talking herself into liking Edwin
Clark, Sara immediately dragged up countervail-
ing arguments.

"If Edwin Clark loved you so much, why did he take up so quickly with someone else?" Sara asked. "I know one thing for certain. Jasper would never run away just because Aunt Hetty made an ugly face."

Jasper suffered ugly faces from Hetty every day and put up with them, just to see Olivia. That certainly ought to be evidence enough of courage!

Hetty sailed into the kitchen waving the elegantly written note to the sender of the flowers.

"I think Edwin Clark will appreciate my fine penmanship. You wouldn't want to risk spoiling such an important impression, Olivia, with your imperfect writing skills."

"Hetty, my writing skills are every bit as good as yours," Olivia protested.

"Hmm," was all Hetty had to say to that. She turned to Sara and changed the subject. "I saw you speaking with Teddy Armstrong last night, Sara."

"Felix says that ever since Teddy's mother died, his father won't speak to anyone in Avonlea."

Prudently, Sara neglected to pass on Mr. Armstrong's opinion about the "hypocrites" in charge of the school. She didn't need to. Hetty already had a low enough opinion of the antisocial farmer.

"A thoroughly irresponsible man, that Jim Armstrong," Hetty scoffed. "Thinks he can teach his son better than a professional teacher."

"Jasper and I met him last week when he found us in his barn," Olivia volunteered, fluffing up some delicate sprays of baby's breath.

Hetty's mouth popped open in shock and a small, squawking sound came out of it.

"Found you in a barn...with Jasper Dale! Thank goodness it *was* Jim Armstrong! What if it had been Clara Potts? Why, you'd have the whole town thinking you were up to some indecency!"

Clara Potts was one of Avonlea's busiest gossips, but she wasn't likely to be found wandering about Lighthouse Point in a rainstorm. Sara, extremely irritated with Hetty's prattle, turned on her heel and marched out of the room. Neither Hetty nor Olivia noticed; they were too busy glaring at each other again.

"All this photographic prancing around..." Hetty continued self-righteously. "It'll be your undoing, Olivia, believe me."

Sara ran out the front door of Rose Cottage and straight off to find her friend, Jasper Dale. She couldn't bear to listen to her aunts squabbling; it was time to take decisive action.

She ran into Jasper not far down the road, driving along in his buggy and looking perfectly miserable. When Sara flagged him down, he was only too glad to dismount and walk beside her. As Jasper led the horse, they discussed the matter that was troubling both their minds.

"You have to sweep her off her feet, Mr. Dale," Sara asserted vigorously. "Just because Edwin Clark's come back to Avonlea doesn't mean you have to let him push you out of the picture."

Jasper shook his head despairingly. He had seen Edwin's fine clothes and the pinkness that had decorated Olivia's cheeks when she spoke to him.

"No, he's an important person, and he's wealthy. You saw everyone the other night... f-fawning all over him. Besides, if Olivia loved him a long time ago, maybe, uh, maybe I shouldn't stand in their way."

This self-sacrificing nobility was too much even for Sara's romantic nature. Besides, she suspected it was only covering up an utter lack of confidence on Jasper's part. He was used to being the Awkward Man; he couldn't imagine that anyone would ever find him attractive. But it would be just awful if Jasper gave up before he had even started!

"But no one can make her laugh like you can," Sara persisted. "Think about that, Mr. Dale."

Jasper did think about it, remembering all the times Olivia's laughter had sparkled around him. His courage welled up mightily inside him. He decided that he would stand in Edwin Clark's way after all.

"All right. All right, I will, I'll do that, Sara Stanley," he announced stoutly. "Goodbye now."

Jasper climbed up into his buggy again, aflame with resolution. Sara beamed encouragingly.

"Remember...the best man always wins!" she called out as he gathered up the reins. Being an idealist, Sara believed in her heart that this was true. Jasper, who had had a lot of experience with not winning things, shook his head.

"I'm not sure about that," he returned, already growing shaky thinking about the effort that would soon be required of him.

Jasper drove away, leaving Sara standing in the road, fighting uneasiness and hoping against hope that Jasper would prevail.

By evening, Jasper had had plenty of time to contemplate the awesome enterprise to which he had committed himself. Demons of doubt tormented him from every direction. Even when he took refuge in his photographic studio, nothing helped.

"Oh, sure. Sweep her off her feet," he mumbled to himself while fiddling with an old photographic plate. "Easier said than done, Sara Stanley."

Jasper had little experience in courting, but he knew one thing for sure—in books, all the best lovers used poetry to overwhelm and conquer the object of their affections. Why, often it only took a few melting lines to have the beloved swooning in a fellow's arms.

Lacking other ideas, Jasper thought he would try some poetry, too. Besides, poetry had the advantage of coming pre-written. If Jasper could only learn a verse or two, he might completely escape the necessity of thinking up flowery words on his own. He cracked open an old, leatherbound book and paged through it until exactly the words to describe Olivia leaped at him from the page.

"She walks in b-b-b..."

He stopped and took an enormous breath to control his stammer. Summoning Olivia's face to mind, he plunged on with the verse.

"She walks in beauty, like the night
Of cloudless climes and starry skies;
And all that's best of dark and bright
Meet in her aspect and her eyes...."

A gush of true emotion rushed up, overcoming Jasper's stutter for once. Forgetting all about himself, he spoke the words softly and clearly—for now he was speaking from his heart. With his head leaning on his hand in the yellow lamplight, Jasper saw Olivia surrounded by stars, and he dared dream of what it would really be like to make Olivia his own.

The next day, bolstered by tender visions and strengthened by the poem now emblazoned on his heart, Jasper drove over to Rose Cottage as early as he dared to try for Olivia. He came laden with camera and tripod, for Olivia had asked him to photograph a lovely stand of blooms right across the road from Rose Cottage. When he and Olivia had climbed over the rail fence and set up the camera in the grassy field, Jasper drew a deep breath and launched into his verse.

Unfortunately, the presence of Olivia in the flesh quite overcame his fortitude and he began to stutter hopelessly.

"...all that's b-b-best...of dark and...b-bright meet in the...aspect of her eyes," he sputtered out, bringing what could have been a tender poem to a sorry end.

Olivia, who hadn't the faintest suspicion that

she was being passionately courted, bent over the yellow blossoms in the long grass. When Jasper trailed into silence, she looked up in surprise. As she did so, Jasper took the picture.

"That's a lovely line for describing black-eyed Susans, Jasper." Then, seeing the high angle of the camera, she frowned. "I hope you didn't get *me* in that photograph."

Getting her in the picture was exactly what Jasper had been doing. Hurriedly, he removed the plate from the camera and shoved it into his photographic box, as if he feared that Olivia might see her own image on its undeveloped surface and realize he meant to cherish the result for life.

"Listen," said Olivia, intent on a fine photograph for the Avonlea *Chronicle*, "why don't we lower the tripod and get a shot of these flowers here?"

With his poem gone awry, Jasper's plan for wooing Olivia had fallen apart completely. He had no idea what to do next, and he certainly couldn't think of a thing to say. By now, his mouth was dry, his hands fumbling and his feet seemed glued to the ground.

What was worse, Olivia didn't even notice his condition. As she tried to help him move the camera, he stepped backward, tripped over a tuft of grass and fell smack into the midst of the black-eyed Susans, taking Olivia with him. When she saw the baffled look on Jasper's face, Olivia began to laugh heartily.

"I wasn't, uh...I wasn't watching what I was doing," Jasper stammered, more upset than ever. "I'm...I'm...I'm sorry. I..."

With Olivia so close and his courtship attempt all shot to pieces, Jasper suddenly lost his nerve altogether. He floundered to his feet.

"I forgot something...a plate, uh, a plate in the fixing solution in my lab. I, uh, I'll be right back, um, ah!"

He rushed to the fence and fell over that too, breaking the top rail as he went. The tumble barely slowed his flight towards his buggy.

"I'll be right back."

In bewilderment, Olivia watched Jasper bolt the field of romance and flee to the solitary refuge of his farm.

Chapter Six

From the vantage point of Rose Cottage, Sara had seen Jasper decamp in confusion, leaving Olivia alone and perplexed in the cow pasture. The sight dealt a telling blow to Sara's faith in Jasper's staying power—and in his ability to sweep Olivia off her feet. She didn't doubt Jasper's feelings for her aunt, but she certainly knew that if Jasper didn't try harder, the field would be left wide open for the swaggering Edwin Clark.

Sara took her worries over to the King farm, where she and Felix swung meditatively on the barnyard gate.

"We've got to stop Edwin Clark from taking up again with Aunt Olivia," Sara was saying as the gate creaked under her weight.

Felix was all for that. He hadn't forgotten how mean Edwin had been at the social.

"I'll say. He cheated Teddy out of a nickel!"

To Sara, this was but one more proof of the unflattering character she knew Edwin was hiding under his phony crocodile smiles. She just couldn't let her Aunt Olivia get mixed up with a man like that!

"Edwin Clark is no good for her. Poor Jasper isn't going to go much further without an awfully big push." Sara looked earnestly at Felix; after all, Olivia was his aunt, too. "Will you help me?"

"I'd love to give Edwin Clark a taste of his own medicine," Felix said vehemently.

With the objective agreed upon, all that was needed was a plan of action. But as Jasper had already discovered, plans were not so easy to come by, especially plans that had some chance of working. The challenge seemed to defeat even Sara's active imagination.

"I wish we could come up with a prescription—a prescription for true love," she sighed, furrowing her brow in earnest but fruitless concentration.

Felix wasn't usually the one to find inspiration, but he suddenly hopped down from the gate, his face split by a huge grin.

"Come on! I've got an idea!"

When Felix told Sara, she was astonished at the daring of it, but it certainly was worth a try. If it worked, it would solve everything in an instant.

As fast as their legs could carry them, the children raced past the red earth of the bluffs and down a crooked path deep into the woods. The path had the wild look of a trail that very few feet had trod. And it came out, at its end, at an even wilder old cabin, with all sorts of curious odds and ends stacked around its walls.

It was true that the path was an untamed one, for Sara and Felix had raced into a place few people in Avonlea would have dared to go. They had come to the lair of Peg Bowen, known far and wide as the Witch of Avonlea.

Peg was a wiry, startling character of indeterminate age and total lack of convention. She had long ago thrown over the traces of society altogether, going where she liked, saying what she liked, beholden to no one. Consequently, the respectable citizens regarded her with scandalized glares, and most of the local children thought she could turn them into squirrels or tabby cats if she had a mind to!

Sara and Felix used to be scared of Peg, too, for Peg was reputed to know all sorts of spells and potions, and she had the most disconcerting habit of appearing out of nowhere and giving the salty side of her tongue to anyone who crossed her. But then, one of Peg's mysterious herbal brews had saved the lives of two schoolmates when they were terribly sick. It was then and there that Sara and Felix decided Peg Bowen was their friend.

They found Peg sitting in front of the cabin humming to herself while she stirred a great iron cooking pot, steaming vigorously over an open fire. Peg wore an old cloth bonnet and her braid of bushy hair stuck out behind. A bit of blanket, with edges all the colors of the rainbow, made Peg a fitting shawl. Her pet crow, which many people thought to be her "witch's familiar spirit," cawed from a pine branch just above her head.

Peg's eyes were already twinkling as the two children crashed into her front yard.

"Sara Stanley and Felix King." Peg chuckled, as if she had been expecting them. "You look like a couple of cupids tied in knots."

The mention of cupids only confirmed Peg's powers in the minds of the children. It was just like Peg to know already what their mission was about. Since there seemed no point in beating around the bush, Sara launched straight into the problem.

"Did you know that Aunt Olivia is really in love with Jasper Dale," Sara demanded of Peg, "except that she doesn't realize it? Poor Jasper, he'll just be devastated if she marries Edwin Clark. She'll go and live in Halifax and live unhappily ever after. We desperately need your help to do something to stop all this!"

At this tall order, Peg peered at the children out of one eye, then the other, looking more than a little amused.

"Well, m'dear, what makes you think I can work that kind of magic? If I could, I'd be married to..." she thought a moment and laughed aloud, "...the Governor General himself!"

Felix's face fell, and Sara began to look desperate. Peg saw that the children really had been depending upon her. From the looks on their faces they needed some powerful magic and needed it fast. Peg screwed up her own face in thought, stood up and picked up an ancient-looking book with frayed pages sticking out around it. She fixed her visitors with grave eyes.

"What you're asking me to do will require the ultimate in thaumaturgy." The children gaped at her, uncomprehending. "Working wonders," she added, to explain.

Peg stroked her chin, hitched up her shawl and launched straight into the making of magic.

"Spring water boiled with cattails," she intoned, dipping an old tin pitcher into the steaming pot beside her. Solemnly, she dipped her fingers into a canister behind her and sprinkled something into the pitcher. "Angelica seeds to ward off the evil spirits."

At the mention of evil spirits, Felix quivered a little. The crow croaked eerily as Peg next added drops from a squat little bottle taken from her pocket.

"Elm sap sprinkled with the pollen of butterfly wings. The potion of love...*breuvage d'amour*," Peg finished, lifting the pitcher high into the dappled sunlight flickering down through the leafy forest canopy overhead.

The crow cawed again, the sound echoing eerily through the woods and pretty well striking Felix and Sara speechless with awe. How often, they wondered, did anyone get to see a love potion created before their very eyes?

"And all you need now," Peg went on, "is to get Olivia to drink the potion before the next time she sees Jasper Dale."

The mention of Olivia brought the reason for the visit back with a jolt. Sara, especially, realized the need for speed. Edwin Clark, at that very moment, could be laying dastardly siege to her Aunt Olivia's heart.

"We'd better hurry. I'll get Jasper to the house right away."

Peg bobbed her head as she picked up a small glass bottle and poured the concoction into it.

"Once Olivia drinks this, she will become betrothed to the very next unmarried man she sees! It tastes very pleasant when mixed with sarsparilla. Olivia won't be suspicious."

To prove it, Peg splashed a small amount of the potion into a battered cup and offered it to Sara.

"Have a sip."

Automatically, without a thought for the powerful forces she was toying with, Sara tasted the mixture. Her eyebrows went up in surprise and approval.

"It's quite nice, Felix. Try some. It's good. Come on, try it."

But Felix, who seemed to have more of his wits about him at the moment, realized Sara was looking straight at him, and stared at the proffered cup in horror.

"You...and me...betrothed?" He took a step backward that almost sent him tumbling into Peg's great cooking pot.

With a start, Sara realized what she had just done. She had just taken a mouthful of a strong love potion—and Felix was the only unmarried male in sight!

Peg giggled as the two children stared at each other in consternation. She was still chuckling as Sara snatched up the bottle of potion and dashed away, Felix at her heels, to deal with the romantic emergency that had driven them to Peg in the first place.

The object of all these machinations, the reluctant knight who needed help to capture his lady fair, was pedaling through Avonlea on his bicycle. Unless he needed his buggy to transport things, the bicycle was Jasper's preferred method of transportation.

Jasper was absent-minded at the best of times.

Today, agitated over his own ignominious flight from Olivia, he was a definite hazard on the road. He had just passed down the main street and entered the covered bridge that crossed the river at the edge of the village. Naturally, he failed to see Edwin Clark driving his buggy at a reckless clip along the road beyond. Jasper had barely got through the bridge when Edwin Clark came towards him, heading for the entrance at such an excessive speed that Jasper almost crashed into his horse. Edwin pulled the rig to a stop just long enough for Jasper to extricate himself. Luckily, no damage had been done to either party.

"You c-c-could hurt someone at that speed," Jasper chided, rescuing his bicycle and straightening up.

With a supercilious glance, Edwin snapped the reins and clattered off, leaving Jasper trying to keep his balance in the middle of the road.

"Inconsiderate oaf!" Jasper growled after his nemesis as he finally mounted his bicycle and wobbled off. "Who does he think he is?" he was still muttering as he finally puffed into his own barnyard and got off his bike. "He could...kill someone. Dangerous man. Oh...oops!"

True to form, Jasper tripped and dropped his bicycle against the barn wall as he tried to park it.

cxcx

"We've got to stop Edwin Clark from
taking up again with Aunt Olivia."

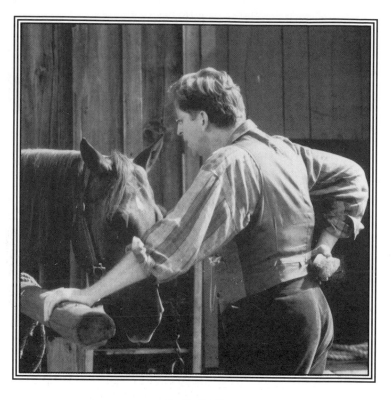

❧❦❧

Jasper struggled mightily to think up
an appropriate speech, and then he began to
practice it on his horse.
"You'll discover many hidden qualities,"
he informed the patient beast.

❧❧❧

"I appreciate all the trouble you've gone to, Sara
Stanley," he said wretchedly, "but I cannot
compete with the ... bouquets from Charlottetown and
the confections from M-M-Montreal...."

ↄ৵ↄↄ

"I love you, Jasper Dale," Olivia declared.
"Well," he gasped, in the throes of romantic ecstasy,
"ain't that the pistol, huh?"

Shaking his head, he went inside, wondering why his whole life seemed to be coming apart at the seams.

Sara raced up to Rose Cottage with no time to spare. Edwin Clark could show up at any moment, forcefully sweeping Olivia off to matrimony and misery in distant Halifax! She ran up the steps and into the house.

"Aunt Olivia? Aunt Olivia, where are you?"

The house was now crammed with flowers, and Hetty, coming out of the parlor after setting out yet another bouquet, answered Sara's question.

"Out walking with Edwin Clark, I do believe," she informed Sara airily, unable to disguise her pleasure.

Hetty went on upstairs, leaving Sara in a state of stark dread in the hall.

"Oh, no," Sara whispered, just as Felix appeared at the front door calling her name. Sara grabbed her cousin.

"Felix! Everything's going wrong. We're running out of time. Edwin Clark's sent Aunt Olivia so many flowers, this house smells like a funeral parlor. She's out walking with him again this afternoon! You get Jasper Dale and bring him over here. I'll wait for Aunt Olivia."

Bent on this momentous mission, Felix turned right around again and took to his heels out the door.

Chapter Seven

When Jasper was troubled in his mind, he usually threw himself into some project that involved a lot of complicated tinkering to distract him from his problem. Today, fighting hard against the image of Olivia gazing up into the face of Edwin Clark, he took to fiddling with a weighted device that would close a barn door by itself. It would be a labor-saving device—very handy for a fellow who regularly forgot to close doors behind himself. The clever weighting mechanism was working fine, but it did a poor job of taking Jasper's mind off Olivia. The corners of his mouth were pulled down, his forehead wrinkled, his expression woebegone in the extreme when Felix came running up, huffing and red in the face.

"Mr. Dale! Mr. Dale!" he shouted, as if half the world were on fire and Jasper Dale the only soul who could do anything about it.

Jasper let go of the door weight, which bounced against the barn wall on the end of its rope.

"Felix?"

"You're needed at Rose Cottage right away," Felix panted. "Aunt Olivia..."

The mere name galvanized Jasper. He took in Felix's panicky state and fell into a fright himself.

"What, wh-what's happened?"

In his hurry to gallop over to Golden Milestone, Jasper's farm, Felix hadn't got round to thinking about what he'd actually say when he got there. Now here Jasper Dale was staring at him, looking as though he wouldn't be able to take his next breath until Felix spilled what the big emergency was.

"She's...um..."

Felix searched frantically around in his mind, knowing he could hardly say a magic potion had just been activated and would erupt in Olivia's life with terrible effect if Jasper didn't get to Rose Cottage when he was supposed to.

"She's taken ill, deathly ill!" Felix croaked, blurting out the only thing that came to him in the heat of the moment.

Poor Jasper! Felix thought the man was going to faint away before his very eyes. But Jasper couldn't allow himself such a luxury, not with Olivia in the throes of goodness knows what horrible complaint! He turned pale, dragged his fingers through his hair and tried desperately to gather his wits.

"Oh, good Lord, um, well, come on, Felix, help me hitch the buggy."

As the two raced into the barn, Jasper forgot all about his ingenious door. It thudded shut with such efficiency that Jasper was caught on the wrong side of it and got whacked smartly on the head as he struggled to rush through.

Inside Rose Cottage, there wasn't the least sign of deathly illness, unless it was the trepidation thumping inside Sara Stanley's bosom. Sara was feeling positively frantic, while Hetty hummed maddeningly to herself in the kitchen, rearranging yet more of Olivia's flowers, and Olivia herself was nowhere in sight.

Keeping a wary eye on her aunt, Sara poured out a glass of sarsparilla from the pitcher and dumped the potion furtively in. She managed this just in time, for at that very moment Olivia stepped into the house through the front door, all bright-eyed and rosy.

"Hetty," she called out from the front hallway, "I just stopped by to tell you that Edwin and I are off to the White Sands Hotel for tea."

At this encouraging development, Hetty beamed hugely and fluttered her fingers at her sister.

"Well, don't dilly-dally then," Hetty advised,

perhaps fearing that Edwin Clark might escape if Olivia did not keep him ever so tightly clutched by the elbow.

With a horrible sinking feeling, Sara heard Olivia's plans. She came rushing into the hallway, the glass of sarsparilla sloshing in her grip.

"No!" she'd exclaimed before she could swallow the word back.

Olivia stopped, much surprised by Sara's agitation.

"What's wrong, Sara?"

A great many things were wrong, in Sara's opinion, but she couldn't say any of them aloud. And now her strategy was all being thrown into confusion by this jaunt to the White Sands with the wrong man for tea.

Sara hastily composed herself and held out the glass of sarsparilla. To its credit, it looked innocent and ordinary, with no hint of the potent sorcery lurking in its depths.

"I thought you might like a cool drink."

Olivia had her mind on the White Sands and was more interested in getting out of the house.

"Oh, no thank you, not right now."

As Olivia started towards the door, Sara dashed to block her way—not an easy task while also balancing a full glass of sarsparilla.

"But I spent a good half hour mixing it from scratch for you," she told Olivia solemnly. The hint of delicate martyrdom in Sara's voice did the trick.

"Oh, I'm sorry." Olivia backpedaled, being tenderhearted and not wanting to hurt Sara's feelings. "I didn't mean I didn't want it." She took the glass and sat down on the edge of hall bench, smiling up at Sara. "Perhaps a cold drink is just what I need. It's very humid out today."

Breath suspended, Sara watched as Olivia downed the contents of the glass without apparent ill effect. But as Sara stepped away from the door, she happened to glance through the window. There was Edwin Clark, large as life, sitting in his buggy by the gate, waiting for Olivia.

"Thank you, Sara, "Olivia was saying as she got up from the bench again. "That was delicious."

As Olivia again made for the door, panic electrified Sara. By any means at all, she had to prevent her Aunt Olivia from opening the door and looking at Edwin Clark. Luckily, Sara was better than Felix at thinking on her feet. She looked pointedly at Olivia's attire.

"Aunt Olivia," she improvised rapidly, "if you're going to the White Sands Hotel, don't you think that you should change into something just a little more...appropriate?"

Caught by surprise, Olivia peered down at her perfectly lovely outfit uncertainly. She did want to fit in at the White Sands Hotel, which was a more elegant place than the Kings were generally used to.

"Oh, I believe I will," she agreed, deciding to err on the safe side. "I'll just tell Edwin I'll be a few more minutes."

Sara placed her body flat against the door panels, prepared to cling and screech if she had to. She smiled weakly.

"Oh, no. I'll tell him. You run along upstairs."

Olivia tilted her head at Sara, beginning to wonder why her niece was acting so strangely. A question rose to her lips, but she thought better of it. With a puzzled glance over her shoulder, she slipped upstairs to change.

As soon as Olivia was safely out of sight, Sara allowed herself a shaky breath of relief before dashing outside to where Edwin stood, impatient as usual, beside his buggy. He looked as vain as ever to Sara, but she managed to keep her dislike from showing in her expression.

"Aunt Olivia said not to wait," Sara told him, looking as sure about it as she could. "She'll meet you there shortly. She's changing her clothes, and she wants to surprise you. You know," Sara leaned forward confidentially, "sort of make a good impression."

Edwin at once looked smug enough to make a parrot seasick. He wasn't keen about going on to the White Sands alone, but now he nodded very agreeably.

"Oh, well, that's fine. You tell her that I'll be waiting for her in the lobby."

Climbing up into his buggy, he drove off, his hat cocked jauntily and his coattails swishing in the breeze. Miss Olivia King, his swagger declared, was practically his.

So far, so good, Sara sighed. Edwin Clark was out of the picture for a while. But where on earth was Jasper Dale?

Worried, Sara peered down the road, searching for a trace of him. She was running clean out of ideas for stalling Olivia. If Jasper didn't show up before Olivia finished changing into another dress, she had no idea what outrageous subterfuge she would have to resort to next!

Jasper was, in fact, speeding towards Rose Cottage as fast as his long-suffering horse would go. His hair stood on end and his driving was so reckless that Felix, trying to cling to the seat beside him, rued the moment he had ever come up with such a crazy story about Olivia. What was the point of stirring up Jasper Dale so violently if neither of them was likely to arrive at Rose Cottage alive!

Since Jasper was in such an emotional state, it was only natural that he should once again meet his nemesis. He tore onto the covered bridge at exactly the same time that Edwin Clark, driving at his usual breakneck speed, clattered onto it from the other side.

Felix gaped, then shouted at the top of his lungs. The warning proved useless. The buggies careened towards each other and met, with the sound of a tremendous collision, smack in the center of the bridge. The frightened neighing of horses and the furious yells of the drivers echoed raucously inside the hollow wooden structure. From the far end of the bridge, Jasper's horse was the only party to exit. It galloped off, dragging the reins and the broken shafts of Jasper's buggy indignantly behind.

"Are you all right?" Jasper called out to Felix as soon as the buggy had rocked to a halt.

Felix, fortunately, was still clutching the seat and was quite unhurt, though he was reeling from the shock of the impact. Edwin Clark, furious about the accident and not the least bit interested in

finding out if anyone was injured, began straight-
away to shout at Jasper.

"Look what you've done! You idiot!" he bel-
lowed, pointing down at the locked wheels and
shaking his fist at the general stupidity of all other
drivers on the road.

For once, Jasper was beyond making apologies.

"This is an emergency," Jasper yelled back, looking ready to pull the locked buggies apart with his
bare hands. "Miss Olivia King has been taken ill!"

If Jasper had had any thoughts of stopping
Edwin's rampage, this fantastic statement certainly did the trick. Edwin's handsome jaw
dropped open.

"Ill? I was there moments ago. She was absolutely the picture of health."

Jasper blinked in confusion and sank back into
the buggy seat. Then he looked hard at Felix.

"Um, that's what Sara told me," Felix mumbled, suddenly scrambling down to the ground as
fast as he could. "Ah...I'll run over to Rose Cottage
to see if she's okay. You'd better fetch your horse,
Mr. Dale."

Before Jasper could even open his mouth again,
Felix was hightailing it down the road, determined
to escape before Jasper could begin grilling him
about his whopping lie.

Abandoned on the bridge with Edwin Clark, Jasper turned back to the problem at hand.

"Now, b-b-back this buggy out..." he ordered Edwin, more anxious than ever to get to Olivia. No matter what Edwin Clark said, Jasper had to see for himself whether she was prostrate with some dread disease or not.

Chapter Eight

Back at Rose Cottage, Sara was still holding the fort and growing more anxious by the minute. Olivia had changed her clothes, smoothed her hair and come back down the stairs again. Now she was trying on hats in front of the hall mirror—and there was still no Jasper Dale in sight!

"I won't be more than an hour," she was telling Sara as she looked critically at a smart straw boater laden with flowers.

Dithering over her choice, Olivia peered through the window towards the front gate, where Edwin and his buggy were supposed to be waiting. The empty road took Olivia by surprise.

"Oh, has Edwin left?" she asked, faintly distressed.

Quickly, Sara did her best to look innocent— which she most certainly was not. She hadn't reckoned on having to explain Edwin's absence.

"He promised he'd be back in twenty minutes," she said, squirming inside at the fresh story she was having to make up. "He wanted to change his clothes, too."

Olivia frowned. She couldn't imagine the self-assured Edwin wanting to change his elegant suit just to have tea. She fixed Sara anew with a troubled eye.

"Are you sure, Sara?"

"That's what he said," Sara lied stoutly, finding out the hard way that one fib led to another and another. "I suppose he just wanted to make a good impression."

Olivia turned back to the mirror and struggled with a hat pin, deciding to wear the flowery boater after all.

"Well, I don't know why I'm fussing so much. I'm only going out to tea with an old friend." Olivia finally got the pin stuck through securely and stepped back to examine her reflection. "What do you think?" she asked Sara.

At this moment there was an urgent knock at the door. Sara showed every sign of melting into a puddle on the floor from sheer relief.

"Perfect," she breathed, knowing that Jasper would adore Olivia even if she appeared in a burlap sack wearing a bird's nest on her head.

Preparing to see the bolt of true love, like a brilliant flash of lightning, pass before her very eyes, Sara clasped her hands expectantly as Olivia pulled open the door. The next instant, Sara choked on her happy sigh. There, standing before Olivia, was not Jasper Dale but only Felix, disheveled from the buggy mishap and looking totally disgusted with life.

"Oh, no, not again," Sara groaned, feeling the charm of the magic potion used up uselessly even as they stood there.

But had Felix arrived even a minute or two later, Edwin Clark would have been the first man knocking at the door. The moment Edwin had got his buggy disentangled from Jasper's, he had turned it right around and raced back to Rose Cottage again to find out what that bumpkin, Jasper Dale, had been talking about. He didn't want to bestow his attentions upon a woman who might turn out to have sickly tendencies.

As soon as Edwin, more than a little put out, pulled up at the gate, Olivia hurried out to meet him. Her cheeks were pink and her steps energetic. She seemed about the liveliest sick person Edwin had ever seen!

"Olivia, you don't look ill at all," he observed, checking her up and down in detail.

"Well, who said I was?" Olivia exclaimed, pausing in bewilderment.

"Why, Jasper Dale."

Now Olivia looked perfectly astonished.

"Jasper? I wonder where he got that idea?" Come to think of it, Olivia thought, a certain niece of her's had been acting very oddly. She turned back towards Rose Cottage. "Sara?"

Sara had gone into hiding behind the front door, mortified at the fiasco that had resulted from her interference.

"Do you know why Jasper would say that?" Olivia demanded. "Sara?"

Sara only shrank further back behind the door, saved from answering by Edwin, who insisted on boosting Olivia up into the buggy seat.

"There you go," he boomed, hopping up beside her. He was determined to whisk her away to the White Sands and into his own influence as quickly as he could.

After Edwin and Olivia had driven off down the road, Sara came out of the house and sat dejectedly on the front steps. Felix followed and plopped down beside her.

"It's a terrible thing we've done," Sara muttered. "I feel sick at making up such lies. Poor Aunt Olivia...poor Jasper."

"Poor me!" put in Felix, who had had his own share of harrowing experiences that day. "How do I tell Father and Mother I'm betrothed to *two* people?"

A furious rattle interrupted the children's gloomy reflections. Oh no! It was Jasper Dale approaching at breakneck speed in his hastily repaired buggy. Both Felix and Sara jumped up in a panic, bent on getting out of his way as soon as possible.

"Come on, Felix," Sara whispered. "I've got an idea."

Felix was only too glad to slip away before Jasper pulled up. Ducking round the corner of the house, under cover of the spirea bushes, the two children quickly vanished from sight.

Jasper arrived in an agitated state, far behind Edwin Clark, who had taken such an unfair head start. Jasper had had to catch his runaway horse, and then improvise some way of attaching the horse to the buggy again. He drove up now with the shafts tied together with hurried knots of rope and a horse with burrs in its tail from the ditch Jasper had had to coax it out of.

Frantically, Jasper half tumbled down from the buggy seat, set out for Rose Cottage, then stopped in his tracks as he began to collect himself. He'd

heard about all the flowers Edwin had been show-
ering upon Olivia. He couldn't possibly go up to
the door without an offering of his own.

Considering this new dilemma, Jasper raked
his fingers through his hair again. Flowers, flowers! Where was a fellow to get flowers when he
was practically standing on a lady's doorstep?

Jasper looked as though he would soon start
pulling his hair out by the roots over all the con-
trary problems that popped up when a fellow
undertook to try his hand at romance. He cast a
look at Hetty's flower beds, but even a braver man
would have stopped short of filching from there.
Back behind his buggy, he scanned the roadside,
finding only a stand of wild asters at his buggy
wheel. The asters were small but vividly purple;
they would have to do. Raggedly breaking off a
bunch, Jasper again set out to assail Rose
Cottage—only to find Hetty King blocking his way
on the porch.

Hetty had seen Jasper wheel up and knew he
could have only one purpose. Like a ferocious
dragon at the entrance to its cave, Hetty had
stepped out of the front door and stood bodily
defending it. Her arms were folded as she watched
Jasper snatch the asters from the ditch and shuffle
forward.

"Sorry, Jasper Dale," Hetty told him triumphantly. "Olivia is off to tea with Mr. Edwin Clark. So you're too late. Good day."

The sight of Hetty, combined with such afflicting news, temporarily stole Jasper's fortitude clean away. The asters fell to his side and he turned around, apparently ready to take flight after a single blow. Swallowing hard, he stopped himself and managed to face Hetty again.

"I was l-l-led to believe by Felix that she was ill, or at least not f-f-f—"

"Feeling?" Hetty snapped, unable to bear Jasper's painful stuttering.

"—feeling very well." Jasper gathered his resolve and got some control over his tongue. "Is she a little under the weather, perhaps?"

The faint wisp of hope in this last question was too much for Hetty. She jerked her head in aggravation.

"Oh, don't be coy, Jasper. You needn't trouble yourself, dreaming up all these feeble excuses just to have the opportunity to speak with Olivia. Time for you to accept the situation as it is and leave Olivia free to pursue—"

"Miss King," Jasper tried to break in, practically shaking his flowers in Hetty's face in an effort to stop the tirade. "Miss King!"

"—a full life," Hetty barreled on, batting the asters away and riding roughshod over Jasper's attempt to interrupt. "There are some things that one cannot change, you see."

Hetty's gloating attitude was too much, even for Jasper. Forgetting everything except his own heart's desire, he shook the asters at her again, this time defiantly.

"Things c-c-can be changed."

"Ha!" was all Hetty had to say to that, whirling to go back into the house.

"No, they, they *will* be changed!" Jasper flung back in desperation.

"Ha!" Hetty practically shouted this time, slamming the front door in Jasper's face.

Crestfallen, Jasper had no choice but to trudge back to his buggy, where he stood in indecision while he fed the hapless asters to his horse.

As it happened, Jasper had good reason to be worried. While he was going through his contortions with Hetty, Olivia and Edwin were arriving at the White Sands Hotel, a grand, many-gabled establishment surrounded by vast manicured lawns sweeping down to the broad beaches from which the hotel took its name.

Edwin escorted Olivia through the empty

conservatory, which also doubled as part of the ballroom when the hotel bustled with guests and entertainment. The ballroom, the scene of many an elegant event, stood empty and quiet, now that autumn was bringing the tourist season to an end. Olivia gazed around musingly at the tall, many-paned windows and the ferns trailing gracefully from their ornate stands.

"One tends to think of the White Sands as being so busy with tourists," she commented slowly, "but I much prefer it when summer's over, and everything's calm and peaceful."

"Yes, so do I, Olivia," replied Edwin, who had never had a thought about the beauty of empty ballrooms in his life.

Edwin was not blind to the significance of the proper setting and the proper mood, though. The opulent ballroom, with no one else around to interrupt, and himself looking doubly rich and handsome reflected in the large, ornately framed mirrors, was perfect. He put on his best, most benevolent face to impress Olivia and put his arm around her shoulders under the arching ceiling. Edwin had decided to campaign in earnest.

"I want to thank you for joining me for tea today," he began, gazing down at Olivia significantly. "I realize that my visiting you out of the blue might seem strange, but, you see, I've loved you ever since I first set eyes on you over ten years ago. I was young and unsure. And I must admit," he smiled somewhat wryly, "Hetty certainly had a way of intimidating suitors."

At the back of her mind, Olivia had been half expecting this, but the actual words threw her into breathless uncertainty. The silken flowers on her hat trembled. Unsure of herself, and not wanting Edwin to read the expression in her eyes, she moved away. Seeing her reaction, Edwin followed, beginning to look more than a little pleased.

"We were like ships passing in the night," he continued, getting warmed up to his rhetoric, "only I can never stop imagining what it would have been like if...if I hadn't left the Island, and if our lives had become intertwined...permanently."

Edwin even managed to put a little quiver into his last few words, conveniently glossing over the fact that when he had skipped the province, he had done it in the consoling company of (rest her soul) Althea Gillis.

Olivia heard the tremor, too, and she turned suddenly around. She had suffered greatly over Edwin's defection and had carried the memory hidden in her bosom all these years. Now that

Edwin seemed to be admitting regrets, she felt she could share hers, too.

"I used to wish that too, Edwin," Olivia whispered, looking up at him with large, troubled eyes. "I cried myself to sleep many a night, wishing..."

Olivia's voice failed her. Faltering, she turned towards the windows, through which the distant beaches and the gray-blue sea could be seen stretching to the horizon.

"Wishing what?" Edwin pressed her, determined not to lose this advantage.

Olivia was only too aware of him standing just at her shoulder in his fine suit, with his finer profile, all his flattering attention fixed on her. She clutched at her handbag without even being aware of what she was doing. Rapidly, a half-embarrassed, half-excited flush climbed her cheeks.

"You make me feel like a ridiculous schoolgirl all over again," she got out shakily.

A tiny, victorious smile crept along Edwin's lips. Then, touching Olivia on the shoulder, he looked as earnest and purposeful as he could.

"Olivia, we can go back to the way we felt about each other then. Tell me...wishing what?"

The chandelier glittered behind Edwin's head like all the tears Olivia had once shed. In the hushed, tremulous silence of the empty ballroom, a hundred yearning memories came flooding back, proving to be all too much for Olivia. She tilted her head towards Edwin Clark.

"Wishing that...I'd find myself in your arms once again."

Never a man to let the opportune moment pass, Edwin immediately swept Olivia into his arms and pressed his lips to hers. His sheer forcefulness overwhelmed Olivia. Forgetting everything else, Olivia closed her eyes and recklessly let herself be whirled away by Edwin's kiss.

Chapter Nine

While Edwin was dallying with Olivia at the White Sands, Sara and Felix were racking their brains wondering how to undo the terrible romantic tangle. There seemed to be nothing for it, they concluded, but to run back to Peg Bowen and confess how they had botched up the magical potion. Felix was especially anxious to get back to Peg. He had a horrible future as a bigamist to escape!

The two arrived at Peg's cabin late in the afternoon and related their sad tale. Gravely listening, Peg sat in front of her steaming cauldron and pondered everything she was told. Periodically, she seemed to have trouble keeping a straight expression on her face.

"Olivia King and you!" she exclaimed to Felix as he told how he had knocked on the Rose Cottage door just at the very moment Sara had got Olivia full of potion and primed to fall madly in love with Jasper Dale.

"I need a new potion to change it," Felix begged, fearing arrest and jail should the authorities ever find out about his waiting line-up of wives.

Peg shook her old cloth bonnet gloomily as if she, too, regretted getting mixed up in the affair.

"Mice, mice, blasted mice..." she mumbled to herself cryptically. "Oh well, it can't be changed now. Children, I have a confession to make."

Felix picked up the fatal tone in Peg's words and fell into a panic.

"What do you mean...it can't be changed?"

"No, lad," Peg lamented, shooting Felix a swift, sidelong glance. "I was thinkin' about it earlier, and I realized I'd made a grievous error. Forgot to include one other active ingredient... powdered mouse bones."

Sara looked relieved. If Peg hadn't got the recipe right, perhaps they had another chance after all!

"Hurry up and make the potion again, Peg. We haven't a moment to lose."

"We?" Felix squeaked, weak with relief at his narrow escape from bigamy and already shaken up by his previous brushes with the occult. "I'm not poking my nose into other people's business ever again. I don't want to be betrothed to anyone, and I bet you Jasper doesn't need any potion to get Aunt Olivia."

If Felix could have known what was just then going on at the White Sands Hotel, he might not have made such a wildly optimistic statement. And Peg, who ought to have been using her magical powers to foil Edwin Clark's machinations, only agreed with Felix.

"Maybe you're right, lad. Fate has a way of throwing things off course. Magic can't force a square block into a round hole, you know."

Understanding—along with a certain disappointment—flew into Sara Stanley's eyes.

"You mean Aunt Olivia and Jasper had better sort out their own lives?"

"Exactly!" cried Felix, imagining that this idea freed him from any more romantic plotting.

Sara, never one to give up, only let out a sigh as she felt a heavier responsibility fall upon her. If the magic potion had turned out to be too good to be true, why then, she'd just have to solve the problem the old-fashioned way—by the use of her wits and her own considerable powers of persuasion.

Sara had an opportunity to get started that very evening, sitting in the parlor beside Olivia. Olivia had come home from the White Sands quite light-headed from her encounter with Edwin in the deserted ballroom. Edwin had treated her to the fanciest tea the hotel had to offer and driven her back to Rose Cottage in such a dashing manner that a number of chickens foraging along the roadsides had barely escaped with their lives. Naturally, Olivia had been unable to hide her excitement from Sara's perceptive eyes, so she had given up and told the whole tale to her niece in the parlor.

"Everything's going so fast, Sara," she confessed, clasping her hands in her lap and peering around at the floral tributes festooning every corner of the room. "All these flowers and all the attention..." Olivia went on, blinking hard. "I feel like a top spinning out of control."

Though she tried to remain calm, Sara's eyes were huge with alarm as she heard about the happenings at the White Sands Hotel. Edwin Clark was a man who was used to getting what he wanted. And now that he had truly mounted the attack, Sara greatly feared her aunt might not have the fortitude to withstand his romantic onslaughts.

"What about Jasper?" Sara demanded, staunchly determined to hold up Jasper's side as much as she could.

Olivia all but wrung her hands.

"Oh, dear, Sara. The thing that worries me the most about Jasper is that he's such a confirmed bachelor. I...I know we've had wonderful times together, and he's kind and gentle and considerate, and he always makes me laugh so. Whereas Edwin is—"

"—rich and boring," Sara declared vehemently. "And he thinks he can buy you, just like his chocolates and his flowers."

"Oh, Sara, I don't give two hoots about the flowers. It's just..." Olivia's voice dropped as she let her memories flood back, "...it's just hard to forget the first person you ever fell in love with. I just want everything to be the way it was a long time ago."

Olivia's face was screwed up in distress—far too much distress for someone who truly wanted to be romanced by Edwin Clark. And Sara certainly wasn't going to defend Edwin.

"But things can't ever be the same as they used

to be," Sara argued. "How can you love him now
when you don't really even know him?"

Leaving Olivia to ponder that profound question, Sara got up and left the parlor. Olivia, looking
vulnerable and alone, stayed behind in the lamplight, battling the thousand doubts that would not
let her rest.

While Olivia spent the night thinking about
Edwin, Jasper Dale spent those very same dark
hours stewing over Olivia. His unfortunate
encounter with Hetty had stung him to the quick,
causing him to discover more gumption hiding
away in his character than Hetty would ever have
dreamed possible. After not getting a single wink
of sleep, he leaped out of bed in the morning
determined to have his say with Olivia at least.

Of course, when a fellow was afflicted with a
terrible stutter, having his say with a lady could be
an almost insurmountable problem. Jasper struggled mightily to think up an appropriate speech,
and then, at dawn, he began to practice it on his
horse.

"You'll discover many hidden qualities," he
informed the patient beast. "I might not have...I
might not have the, the aura that is this Edwin
Clark, but neither does he have the aura that is,

um... Olivia, what, what I want to say... You'll discover many hidden qualities...I'm...oh..."

Poor Jasper! The harder he tried, the bigger the verbal snarl he got himself into. He ground to a halt, tearing his fingers through his hair yet again and grabbing the horse's halter to keep it from trying to escape.

Back at Rose Cottage, things were in a much more dangerous state than even Jasper could have imagined. Sara came down the stairs just in time to hear voices from the garden. Peeping out the door to the veranda, she saw Edwin and Olivia underneath the rose trellis. Dismay raced through her. How did that man manage to be at Rose Cottage every time Olivia turned around?

"Olivia," Edwin was saying, "I thought we could drive along the coast, stop at the cove. Perhaps, after lunch, we could go for a walk."

Olivia beamed widely, all her uncertainties swept away by Edwin's determined charms.

"Oh, that sounds wonderful, Edwin."

Edwin straightened, looking very complacent about his success with Miss Olivia King.

"Good. See you at the White Sands at four o'clock."

Sara shut the door and frowned in consternation. All kinds of irreversible things could happen while Edwin and Olivia traipsed off on a picnic. Picnics could be so dangerously romantic; Sara didn't even want to think about it. She imagined Edwin and Olivia holding hands and strolling across the beautiful, windswept cove all aglow with banks of autumn flowers. Picnics were notorious settings for the springing of marriage proposals! And once Olivia had accepted Edwin, the damage could never be undone.

Once again, Sara knew she had to have a word with Jasper Dale.

Chapter Ten

Driven, once again, to direct action, Sara sped out the side door and made for Jasper Dale's farm. Straight to the barn she raced, blond hair flying, and pulled open the door.

"Mr. Dale! Mr. Dale!" she called out urgently, trying to locate the elusive man.

As she'd expected, she finally found him in the studio he had fixed up in the barn loft. He was hunched over his desk making a poor pretense of working. She began talking at once, as fast as she could talk—which, with Sara Stanley, was very fast indeed. She had to explain what had happened the day before.

"Felix told that whopper just to get you to Aunt Olivia's so that Peg's love potion would get her to marry you. We'd all be horrified if she ever left to marry Edwin Clark, maybe even leave Avonlea forever."

If Sara expected Jasper to be bowled over by this storm of explanations, she was quite mistaken. Jasper was already knocked over in spirit about as far as he could go. His inability to make an amorous speech, even to his horse, had wrecked the last scrap of self-confidence he had been able to muster. Instead of setting off to win Olivia, he had retired to his studio in the depths of defeat and despair.

"I appreciate all the trouble that you've gone to, Sara Stanley," he said wretchedly, "but I cannot compete with the...bouquets from Charlottetown and the confections from M-M-Montreal. Besides, she probably still loves him."

Sara wasn't buying a single one of these excuses. It was about time Jasper Dale stopped hiding out and opened up his eyes.

"Aunt Olivia's frightened," she told him forcefully. "I'm sure the only reason she'd even consider Edwin Clark is because she thinks you'll never ask her to marry you. She's worried you're a confirmed bachelor."

And everyone else in Avonlea would have sworn to this opinion—except Jasper himself. Confirmed bachelors were usually fellows who suffered the pangs of love in tortured silence rather than risk popping the big question to the objects of their adoration. There was a penalty for such backwardness, of course. Confirmed bachelors spent the rest of their lives alone, listening to the clock tick while their hair turned slowly gray. Before Olivia had come along, Jasper had resigned himself to such a fate. Now that he had known her laughter and companionship, the prospect of such future solitude seemed too dismal to be faced.

"Um, well, that isn't exactly true," Jasper mumbled, thinking how much of his life he would gladly change if only Olivia King would share it with him.

"I know that," Sara replied, pacing ever more restlessly about the studio, "but Edwin Clark is in the garden right now, maybe even proposing to her. You have to tell her yourself that she's making a mistake, that you're not the man you appear to be. Show her that you love her." Sara paused dramatically, then added, "This may be your only chance."

Something about Sara Stanley could brace the most dejected spirit. Besides, she had just dropped a vivid picture into Jasper's mind of Edwin Clark swiftly overpowering Olivia with his flood of fast talk and his slick, sharklike smile. Jasper suddenly dropped the bit of photographic paper he had been dolefully toying with and leaped to his feet. No matter what the cost to himself, he couldn't abandon Olivia to such a fate.

"You're right. I will," he spluttered, knocking over his stool as he stepped backward. "Things will be changed!"

"Sweep her right off her feet!" Sara exhorted, breaking into an enormous grin herself.

After a morning of paralyzing discouragement, Jasper suddenly acted as though he were racing to a fire. And, in a way, he was, for Edwin Clark proposing to Olivia was an emergency of the first degree. He prodded his horse out of its comfortable doze in the barnyard, flung its harness on and hitched it to the buggy, nearly tying the both of them into a knot in the process. Soon Jasper was racing over to Rose Cottage, Sara clinging to the seat beside him.

Even with all the rushing, they barely arrived in time. Across the road from where Jasper pulled up, Edwin Clark was helping Olivia into his own shiny buggy.

In contrast to Edwin's immaculate suit, Jasper

had been caught in his old work vest and hadn't given a thought to combing his hair. The breakneck ride over to Rose Cottage had left him looking like a wild man, with his hair sticking out and his collar all askew.

"Hold on there," Jasper called out to Edwin and Olivia. "Just wait there, Mr....uh...Clark," he ordered with surprising firmness as he levered himself down to the ground. "Miss King, I have something...uh, I have something that..."

Faced with a real Olivia and not just his imagination, Jasper's tongue again betrayed him.

Seeing Jasper in danger of freezing up at what was probably the most crucial moment in his life, Sara leaned down from the buggy seat to whisper in his ear.

"Tell her something has happened to you."

"Something important has happened to me," Jasper called to Olivia, grasping gratefully at Sara's words. "I need to speak to you...alone."

Edwin, determined to get Olivia away from this persistent fool, got out his pocket watch pointedly.

"Olivia...our plans..."

Ignoring him, Olivia got down from the buggy and moved towards Jasper. Seeing his request actually being obeyed, Jasper began to look dangerously speechless again.

"Tell her...tell her that you love her," Sara prompted hastily in a smothered voice, "and that you want her hand in marriage. Don't worry, Mr. Dale, she'll choose you. I know she will. Just tell her."

By now, Olivia had glided right up to Jasper and was looking at him with a sort of questioning eagerness. In spite of all the temptations Edwin was offering, she seemed very glad to see her old companion.

"What's wrong, Jasper?"

Faced with the big moment, Jasper swallowed hard, his Adam's apple bobbing violently up and down several times. He hemmed and hawed so much that Sara wondered whether she would have to do the proposing on his behalf. But, at last, Jasper found his powers of speech.

"I...I need you to choose...uh, no...I need you to ask...no, no...I want to ask you for—"

"Mr. Dale!" broke in another voice. It was Felix, urgently shouting from afar.

Jasper was concentrating so hard on his message that he didn't even hear the boy.

"I want to ask you for your hand in marriage," he got out in a burst. Despite his little round spectacles, all the profound feeling welling up inside him shone from his eyes.

Before Olivia could even react, Felix came pounding up and thrust himself between them. His face was paper-white with fright and his neck bore scratches, as though he had been tearing through the brush without a single thought to shielding his own hide.

"Mr. Dale, Teddy Armstrong! Teddy Armstrong was playing tag with a bunch of kids in the wood!"

"I've loved you for some time," Jasper said to Olivia over Felix's head. All Jasper could think of was how lovely Olivia's hair looked gleaming in the sunlight, and how he might just perish on the spot should she refuse him.

"He fell through the cover of an old well," Felix yelped, completely disregarding the tender moment he was interrupting. "We've been calling to him, but he won't say anything. I think he might've broken his neck or drowned!"

This drastic revelation finally broke the spell of Olivia's presence and got Jasper's attention. One look at Felix told him that this was more than some mere playtime drama. Teddy Armstrong really was lying at the bottom of a well in mortal danger.

Responding to the gravity of the situation, Jasper jerked into action. Without even knowing what he was doing, he automatically took command. He shook one hand in Sara's direction.

"Uh, Sara, go and fetch a lamp."

Sara leaped down from the buggy seat and streaked for the house. Getting his mind even further in gear, Jasper turned to the back of the buggy and scanned it for tools. Since Jasper's buggy was always full of assorted odds and ends, Jasper was able to pull out a shovel, a coil of rope and, after a second's thought, a horse collar he had meant to take into the village for repair.

He handed the shovel to Felix to carry. Felix had been hopping from foot to foot the whole time, growing more frantic by the second.

"Um, Felix...here. Now, why don't you show us where he is!"

Grabbing the shovel with both hands Felix took off immediately into the woods, paying no heed to the bushes that tore at his clothes, with Jasper and Olivia at his heels.

Edwin Clark now found himself standing uselessly by his buggy. Realizing that there was an emergency at hand, and gawky Jasper Dale was taking charge of it, Edwin finally came to life. He couldn't afford to have Jasper upstaging him here. Grabbing a pickax, which was all that was left in the back of Jasper's buggy, Edwin started reluctantly into the woods, too.

Chapter Eleven

Jasper and Olivia, followed belatedly by Edwin, went crashing after Felix through clutching bushes, around tree trunks and over mossy fallen logs. Jasper, for all his usual awkwardness, proved he could run like a deer, even laden with rope, a horse collar and the effects of a recent marriage proposal. Olivia rushed along nimbly behind, lifting up her hems to avoid snags. Edwin, stubbing his toes and cursing under his breath, brought up the rear.

In a few moments, they all arrived at a knot of scared-looking boys of about Felix's age who were staring down into a deep, black hole.

The hole was in the middle of a lot of old, splintered boards—the broken top that had covered the old well. The well was so covered with leaves and moss that it blended almost perfectly with the forest floor, and it was no wonder that Teddy Armstrong hadn't seen it.

Edwin, stomping up behind the rest, made an effort to snatch the role of leader away from Jasper.

"There it is," he barked, pointing at the well as though no one else had had the wit to see it. "Stand back, now. Let's take care of it."

Jasper flung out a cautioning arm against whatever rash action Edwin had in mind.

"Let's have a look." He bent over the hole and peered in. "Teddy!" he called out, "Teddy!"

No answer came back, and little could be seen in the blackness beyond the splinters.

"Stand aside!" Edwin Clark made another attempt to shoulder Jasper out, but Jasper already had a grip on the edge of the crumbling well cover.

"Felix! Look out," Jasper warned as he heaved the entire cover off to the side. "Teddy!" he called out again, but the hole was even deeper and more silent than before.

By now, just about everyone, including Olivia, was on their hands and knees around the well rim, half in danger of falling in themselves. Felix and the other boys looked terrified, partly for Teddy and partly in fear that the adults would blame them for the accident. Sara, who had just that moment come rushing up with a lantern grabbed from beside the woodshed door, leaned over into the well as far as she could.

"I can't see him moving," she gasped, having made out a faint, motionless outline at the bottom of the hole.

"Teddy," Felix pleaded vainly, "say something!"

Teddy refused to oblige, even when Olivia called out his name, her voice echoing plaintively in the musty well shaft.

What was needed, immediately, was some light on whatever disaster was down below. Jasper, fortunately, had some matches in his pocket. He gave them to Felix and told him to light the lantern. As soon as Felix's shaky hands had put fire to the wick, Jasper was tying the handle to the end of the rope he had brought.

"Here, hold this," he commanded, shoving the rope at Edwin. "Let's lower the lantern."

Carefully keeping the glass sides of the lantern from banging on the stones lining the well shaft, Jasper lowered it down and down into the cavity. As it dropped, its light revealed a small, sprawled form at the very bottom, horrifyingly still.

"I can see him, Mr. Dale," Felix burst out, shivering. "It's a long way down."

Jasper knew that perfectly well. He nodded his head towards the second, larger coil of rope lying on the ground beside him.

"Felix, pass me that large line."

Olivia was looking more and more distressed at Teddy's stillness. It simply wasn't natural for a boy to lie as inert as that. "Hold on, Teddy," she called down encouragingly, even though Teddy showed no sign of being able to hear. They all ought to be thankful, she supposed, that the well was dry and there hadn't been any water to drown the lad.

Jasper began to lower the larger rope into the well. Olivia cast a sidelong glance at Edwin, who was sitting back on his heels watching the proceedings. Catching Olivia looking at him, Edwin roused himself for another stab at command.

"That's it," he growled in the direction of Jasper's rope-lowering efforts. His attempts at an air of authority didn't have the least effect upon Jasper, or anyone else, save to make Olivia faintly embarrassed.

"All right, now give me the horse collar," Jasper ordered, waving one hand beside him in readiness for the item.

With bad grace, Edwin handed over the cracked and heavy leather collar, which Jasper laid down on the well rim in readiness for use. Sara was staring down at the motionless form far below.

"Someone will have to go down and get him," she murmured, daring to state what was obvious to everyone by then.

The moment for heroism had arrived—and there were only two candidates for the job. Jasper and Edwin exchanged a glance. One of them would have to climb down into the dank shaft to retrieve the boy.

Edwin Clark made no move at all, his face hard and blank.

"Edwin," Olivia urged, appalled by the reaction of the man who had seemed so gallant to her in the safety of the White Sands Hotel.

Not even the huge, dark eyes of Olivia could move Edwin. It was clear that he considered Teddy someone else's responsibility and wanted no part of his rescue—at least, no dangerous part. Immediately, Jasper Dale stood up and started tying a rope around his own waist. Sara leaned as far as she dared over the well rim.

"Teddy, can you hear me? We're coming to get you."

Dragging a heavy branch across the well top to loop the rope over, Jasper stepped to the edge. Olivia forgot all about Edwin.

"Be careful, Jasper," she whispered, fixing all her attention on the hero of the moment.

With a bit of a nod, Jasper climbed bravely into the narrow hole. He lowered himself hand over hand along the rope and used his feet to keep himself from scraping against the rough stone walls inside. His arms were burning in their sockets as he neared the lantern glowing in the dimness below.

Soon, to the audible relief of the watchers above, Jasper landed with a thud beside Teddy. The lantern sat crookedly, casting a pale circle of light on the injured boy. Teddy was still sprawled in the moldy debris at the bottom, unconscious and totally unaware of the effort mounted to rescue him.

"Is he all right, Jasper?" Olivia called down anxiously, her voice echoing against the stone walls.

Jasper couldn't tell her. He crouched down in that small space and wiped Teddy's forehead with the boy's cap, which was lying nearby. Swallowing, he remembered that same cap perched on Teddy's head that day on Lighthouse Point when he had impulsively snapped Teddy's picture.

"There now," he soothed, overcoming the tightness in his throat, "let's have a look at you."

The look revealed a whopper of a gash gleaming in the lantern light. Teddy must have given his head a terrific wallop as he fell. Jasper could get no response at all from him. He felt for the boy's pulse.

"He's alive," Jasper shouted up, relief and worry fighting in his voice. "Go fetch Dr. Blair and find the boy's father. Tell them to meet us at Rose Cottage."

At Jasper's command, two of the waiting boys who had been playing with Teddy sprang up and sped off through the trees as though their feet had wings. They were exceedingly glad to be of any use at all.

Jasper turned back to Teddy, quickly feeling his arms and legs to see if anything was broken. When each limb proved to be straight and firm, there still remained the problem of getting the boy to the surface. Luckily, the one thing Jasper was never short of was inventiveness.

"Throw that collar down," he called up to the circle of waiting faces above.

"What?" Edwin asked, looking cluelessly at the collar. "Where do you want it?"

"Just drop it," Jasper snapped. "Drop it, man, drop it."

Chastened slightly by Jasper's tone, Edwin picked up the horse collar and dropped it down into the well. Jasper grabbed it before it could hit Teddy and tied an end of rope to it.

"What's he doing, Aunt Olivia?" Sara wanted to know as she watched Jasper fiddling with something she always thought belonged on a horse.

She soon found out. As soon as the knot was secure, Jasper lifted Teddy very gently up and slipped him through the wide oval.

"He's in the collar," Felix cried, amazed at Jasper's quick thinking.

Jasper had put the horse collar around Teddy's body, with Teddy's arms outside it. The collar proved exactly the right shape to take the boy's weight without hurting him or letting him slip out.

"Don't worry, boy," Jasper murmured to the unconscious lad. "We'll have you out of here in a minute."

He leaned back and waved his arm at the watchers, this time ignoring Edwin in favor of the more caring face beside Felix's.

"All right, Olivia, get ready. Here he comes."

By tying the rope to the top of the horse collar and using the branch above as a primitive pulley, Jasper hauled Teddy rapidly to the top of the well, where Olivia and Edwin quickly grabbed the boy to take him from the collar.

"Gently," instructed Jasper, worrying that someone up there would inadvertently jar Teddy's wounded head.

"Got him," exclaimed Edwin, trying to look manly as he made a grab for the boy. It was Olivia who really got hold of Teddy and lowered him to the ground.

"It's all right now, Teddy," she murmured. "You're safe now."

Sara was considerably shaken up when she saw the boy up close. Teddy was a terrible ashen color, and the gash on his head looked shocking in the sunshine.

"Ted...?" She faltered and began again. "Is he going to be all right?"

Edwin, now that the boy had been pulled out of the well into the light of day, could only think of his interrupted excursion with Olivia and the dirt he now had all over his good clothes. He gave vent to a burst of irritation, addressing not only the unconscious Teddy but Felix and the other lads still standing around.

"You dimwit boys shouldn't play around here in the first place. I hope that teaches you a lesson about staying off of other people's property."

It is at unguarded moments like this that a man's true personality emerges. Edwin had already shirked the chance to rescue Teddy, preferring his own comfort to the boy's safety. Unable to help himself, the spurt of selfishness and bad temper had come bursting out of him. The speech proved a grave mistake on Edwin's part. It had little effect on the boys, but it caused Olivia to rise slowly to her feet, openly aghast at the callousness of Edwin's remarks.

There was no time to argue with Edwin, however. Teddy needed help and needed it fast. Once again, it was Jasper to the rescue. After pulling himself up out of the well, it was a wonder his arms had any strength left in them. Yet, as soon as he struggled over the rim and got to his feet, he was the one who swept Teddy up in his arms and began to run, the rest of the party following behind, towards Rose Cottage and help.

Felix, having only his own fright to carry, got there first and clattered up the front steps, yelling, "Aunt Hetty! Aunt Hetty!" at the top of his lungs.

"Merciful heavens," Hetty cried when she came running and saw the limp child against Jasper's chest. She had been forewarned by Sara and the arrival of Dr. Blair, but she certainly hadn't expected anything as serious as this.

Dr. Blair was at Hetty's heels as Jasper ran up the steps, followed by Olivia, Sara, Felix, Edwin and some of the other boys who had been playing in the woods. Hetty quickly made room so they could all get in the door.

A great vase of Edwin's flowers was rudely

whipped from the kitchen table along with the embroidered tablecloth. Quickly, Jasper laid Teddy down on the polished surface so that the doctor could get a decent look at him.

"His pulse seems quite strong," Jasper informed the doctor. "I don't think anything's broken."

"Hetty, get some hot water," Dr. Blair ordered, pulling his black bag open and taking control.

Hetty sped off to obey while Dr. Blair bent over Teddy's head, looking at the gash.

"Well, let's see how bad this wound is."

Head wounds were tricky things, and Dr. Blair at once began a careful examination.

"Could be a severe concussion," Jasper speculated, revealing that he had done his own reading on medical subjects.

Behind them, Edwin Clark again stood looking impatiently at his watch. Anyone who married him would soon come to realize what an important part Edwin's watch played in his life. Edwin made sure as little of his time as possible got wasted on annoying exercises—such as pulling boys from wells. He found it insufferable to have been upstaged by that gawking joke of a man, Jasper Dale, and all Edwin wanted, right then, was to get out of Jasper's vicinity.

"Jasper," Dr. Blair ordered, turning naturally to

the person who seemed to be most in charge, "get everyone out of here." Teddy's friends and rescuers were more of a distraction than the doctor wanted just then.

Jasper faced the worried group behind him and made waving motions. Now that the immediate emergency over, Jasper came back to himself, aware that he was caught in a roomful of people and stood not three feet from the woman he had just asked to marry him. For the first time since Felix had come shouting up to Rose Cottage, Jasper began to stutter.

"Um...everyone, you'll h-h-have to leave..."

Jasper didn't even dare look at Olivia. His face grew hot behind his spectacles, and he showed every sign of getting ready to trip over the kitchen chairs. Olivia, however, couldn't take her eyes off him, even though he had twigs sticking out of his hair and had popped most of the buttons off his vest during the ordeal of the climb.

"Thank you, Jasper," murmured Olivia admiringly as she turned to leave the room. "You were very brave."

Olivia hadn't even bothered to glance at Edwin as she left. Edwin cast Jasper a disdainful scowl. The kitchen door shut behind the lot of them, leaving Jasper blinking unsteadily in the wake of Olivia's words. Then Teddy moaned, and Jasper stepped swiftly over to help at Dr. Blair's side.

Chapter Twelve

The moment the door had closed behind him, leaving Jasper inside, Edwin squared his shoulders, puffed out his chest and set off to take Olivia in hand. He certainly hadn't missed Jasper's advances to Olivia just before Felix had interrupted, and he supposed Jasper Dale's stock might be dangerously high right now, after the fellow had clambered down that cobwebby well and dragged that silly boy back to the surface. Edwin decided he had better make his move quickly before anyone else decided to cast sheep's eyes at the desirable Miss King.

Olivia had a thousand tumultuous thoughts of her own to deal with and hardly gave a thought to where she was going until she suddenly found herself in the Rose Cottage garden with Edwin Clark stepping abruptly in front of her.

"Olivia," he began when she had come to a halt, "I know this has all been most unsettling, but there's something I wanted to tell you earlier."

"Edwin..." Olivia protested uneasily, with a

sudden suspicion of what Edwin was going to say.

Ignoring her, Edwin rumbled on. He was a man whose time was valuable. He had already prolonged his stay in Avonlea on account of Olivia. His picnic plans had been ruined. Now he would have to say, in the modest Rose Cottage garden, what he had planned to say at the magnificent cove with the Atlantic breakers rolling in. He cleared his throat and affected a suitably humble and supplicating pose.

"I...I have admired and respected you for so long that I came today prepared to ask for your hand in marriage."

Edwin managed, just barely, to insert a pleading quiver in his voice. To prove his claim, he reached into his waistcoat pocket and produced a blue velvet box. Significantly, he popped back the lid to reveal a ring—a big, glittering ring that was probably worth more than Jasper Dale's whole farm. He then paused, waiting for this scintillating bauble to dazzle Olivia.

"I'd give anything in this world to have you for my wife," he continued. Unlike Jasper, he had absolutely no trouble in remembering set speeches, even one totally lacking in originality. "It would be a wonderful life, and I would be the happiest of men, Olivia, contented, proud, honored."

Olivia was quite bereft of speech. She had led ten years of uneventful life since Edwin left—and now, to get two proposals of marriage practically within an hour of each other! How was a woman to deal with it all?

"Oh, Edwin," was all she could manage, "you take my breath away...."

Neither Edwin nor Olivia noticed Hetty, who was watching from a prime vantage point behind the curtain of the window nearest the garden. At the sight of the ring box, her eyes popped wide, and it was all she could do to restrain herself from cheering out loud.

"I'm sure this all seems sudden," Edwin was saying, taking it for granted that Olivia was being swept off her feet by his generous and desirable offer. "I'm asking that you consider accepting this ring as a token of my commitment and esteem."

Just as Edwin held out the ring to Olivia, Sara walked around the corner of the veranda and came, unsuspecting, upon the scene. Stifling a groan, she stopped in her tracks and managed to stay inconspicuously motionless. It was only too obvious what Edwin Clark was up to.

Olivia, happening to glance in agitation past her suitor, caught sight of Sara. The girl's eyes were huge with reproach and full of urgent, gloomy questions about what Olivia intended to do. At the very least, Sara thought, Olivia ought to slip through the garden gate and take to her heels down the road!

Edwin took another step towards Olivia, thrusting the ring closer and closer, as if he expected to hypnotize her with its sparkle. Inside Rose Cottage, Hetty pulled the curtain back further and further as, in the suspense of the moment, she all but forgot about trying to be discreet.

"Please take it," Edwin urged, wondering why Olivia wasn't jumping at the opportunity he was offering, "and think about whether or not you'll be my wife."

Olivia looked at the dazzling stone and swallowed hard. She was very short of practice when it came to dealing with determined, overconfident suitors. She put out a hand to ward off the ring box.

"I'm afraid I can't accept your ring, Edwin. I'm afraid I just can't recapture the past as easily as you can."

For once, it was Edwin's turn to be speechless. He had expected Olivia to consider herself the luckiest of women and collapse straight into his arms. Her refusal astonished him, and he advanced yet another step with the ring.

"Olivia, you don't mean that!"

Unfortunately for Edwin Clark, Olivia did mean it. She stood her ground steadfastly in front of him and glanced up, her eyes at last free from the doubt and confusion that had been clouding them ever since Edwin's arrival.

"I'm sorry," she whispered.

And with that, Olivia slipped past Edwin and walked swiftly away through the autumn garden. Sara let out a great sigh of relief, not caring whether Edwin knew she had been watching or not.

The curtain on the Rose Cottage window fell back into place with a jerk as a scandalized Hetty dropped it. At that moment, Hetty fully believed her younger sister was not only a fool, but mad as well. How dare she make it possible for every gossip in Avonlea to taunt Hetty with the story that Olivia had twice in a row lost out on a rich husband!

As for Edwin, he was left standing with both his ring box and his mouth hanging open. Seeing Olivia disappear around the corner of the house, he stomped off towards his buggy. The last anyone saw of him was a cloud of red dust rising from his wheels as he tore off into the sunset in stiff-necked, outraged pride.

Dr. Blair, having satisfactorily bandaged Teddy's head, had him put to bed in one of the spare bedrooms at Rose Cottage and recommended rest until he recovered fully from the bump he had taken. The doctor was checking on the boy when Jim Armstrong, who had been working in the fields and not easy to find, came storming into the house without so much as a knock and grabbed Dr. Blair by the arm.

"What have they done to my boy?" he demanded, as fiercely as though the inhabitants of Rose Cottage had been plotting to chop Teddy up in pieces for a stew.

"Calm down, Jim," Dr. Blair said, prying his arm free. "He's had a bad fall, but he's all right. Jasper saved his life."

Dr. Blair pointed to Teddy, asleep in the bed and watched over by Jasper Dale. Jasper jumped up and stood back as the big man crossed the room and sank down into a chair beside his son. With the white bandage swathing his head and his lashes resting on his cheeks, Teddy looked very small and vulnerable. A little shakily, Jim Armstrong touched his son's cheek.

"Teddy shouldn't have been playing with those boys," he growled out, still angry.

"Well, he didn't know there was a well there," Jasper put in, knowing all about what it was like to be a lonely lad longing for some company. "He was just having a good time with friends. Go easy on him, Mr. Armstrong. He's a fine boy."

Underneath all the bluster, Jim Armstrong was mightily relieved to see Teddy fast asleep and apparently all in one piece. His anger fell away and he let out a sigh. He was a lot more shaken up than he had been letting on.

"I'll grant you that. You don't know how much you care for a body till you nearly lose 'em."

Jasper gulped hard, for he found himself rather in the same position with Olivia. He hadn't been able to speak to her since Teddy's accident, and he certainly hadn't been party to the events in the garden with Edwin. All he had to go on now was the small smile Olivia was sending him over Jim Armstrong's head as she paused for a moment in the doorway to check on Teddy.

Chapter Thirteen

Being a resilient little fellow, Teddy regained his feet in a gratifyingly short time. When he was ready to go home from Rose Cottage, his father came to pick him up. On their way, they had a stop to make at Golden Milestone to express their thanks for all that Jasper had done. Soon, they found themselves in Jasper's photographic studio, along with Olivia, who had accompanied them there.

The sight of Olivia produced assorted shades of color under Jasper's collar, for he hadn't been in her company since Teddy had been pulled from the well. Intensely aware of her rustling dress and her maddeningly unreadable gaze, he felt altogether flustered.

Jasper turned to the Armstrongs to give them the present he had planned. Olivia looked on, enjoying a memory, as Jasper handed Jim Armstrong a framed photograph of Teddy and his shaggy black dog, Rufus. It was none other than the picture, jam smears and all, that Jasper had snapped the day he and Olivia had taken shelter in the Armstrong lean-to.

"There you go...Jim," Jasper announced, thoroughly pleased with the way he had captured the boy in the photo.

Jim Armstrong took the photo awkwardly into his big hands and gazed at it, pleasure spreading across his rough features.

"Huh...thank you, Jasper," he got out awkwardly, for he had not had many occasions to thank folks for their favors.

Jasper bent over Teddy, whose head was still bandaged and whose face was now colorful with bruises from the fall.

"And you'll be looking as good as this again any day now," Jasper promised, pointing to the picture.

As Jasper passed Teddy a candy from his own private supply, Jim contemplated the photograph, probably the first and only one ever taken of the boy. Rough man though he was, he couldn't get over the simple freshness and charm of the boyish face looking out at him. He had never guessed that a mere picture printed on paper could clutch at a fellow's heart like that. All his gruffness vanished in a burst of fatherly pride.

"That really is him, isn't it?" he beamed, smiling for the first time since Jasper had met him. "You got a cheeky look about you, Ted. Ha, ha, and a blueberry turnover. Always thinking of your stomach."

Recalling the strange chain of events that had led to Teddy's rescue, the big man paused to look ponderingly at Jasper and Olivia.

"You know," he murmured slowly, "if it hadn't rained that day, and if you hadn't used my lean-to for shelter, Teddy might not be here now. It was like it was...I don't know how to say it...."

"Preordained?" Jasper supplied, showing that he had some pretty fancy words in his vocabulary, despite his stutter.

"That's it...preordained," exclaimed the farmer, thinking it a corker how Jasper could hit upon the idea just like that. It would certainly be the last time Jim Armstrong every thought of a camera as bad luck.

"Things have turned out exactly as they were meant to," Olivia added. Privately, she smiled over just how many more things had turned out than Jim Armstrong suspected.

Jasper dared a nervous glance at Olivia and found the corners of her mouth turned up in a smile. Teddy and his father grinned at each other and at their benefactors.

That day, much of the bitterness that had gripped Jim Armstrong since the death of his wife seemed to pass. He enjoyed talking to Jasper, and even took an interest in looking at his photographic equipment.

"Tell Miss King," he said to Olivia as he and Teddy were leaving, "I'll be sending Teddy back to school. The boy's got better things to be doing than running around in the woods and getting into trouble. If a fella wants to play with his friends, he can do it in the schoolyard."

After Teddy and his father left, Jasper found himself all alone with Olivia. He found the prospect so unsettling that he hemmed and hawed and finally bolted downstairs to hitch up the horse and buggy. With the Armstrongs gone on their way, it obviously fell to him to take Olivia home.

Olivia watched this performance with fond amusement. In fact, the laughter she valued so much with Jasper Dale seemed almost to dance on her lips. When the buggy was pulled up outside, she descended from the photographic loft without comment and climbed up into the seat.

Having Olivia squeezed in next to him almost made Jasper drop the reins over the dashboard. The horse, deciding to take some initiative in this affair, set out in the direction of Rose Cottage anyway, leaving its owner to regain what equilibrium he could along the way.

Olivia still wasn't saying anything, although her hand grasped Jasper's elbow for balance every time the buggy hit a rut in the road. Though Jasper didn't dare look sideways, he did begin to gather the scraps of his courage back together. After all, Edwin Clark had left the neighborhood in a hurry right after Teddy's accident, taking, rumor had it, a very grand engagement ring with him.

Jasper's heart swelled inside him as he thought about the huge, unanswered question hovering between himself and Olivia. Olivia might have been silent since Edwin left, Jasper reasoned, but she hadn't exactly been driving him away with sticks! Perhaps...oh, just perhaps, there might still be some shred of hope.

Almost unable to help himself, Jasper began to talk, impelled to share with the woman beside him his dearest dreams.

"It'll take time to build up my photographic business," Jasper was saying as the buggy swayed along. "I'd like to be a photographic historian and travel all across Canada...and perhaps, to be able to buy," he ventured, "two train tickets.... And security. I'd like to offer security with my love."

Jasper's voice didn't falter with the last word, even though his gaze remained firmly fixed between the horse's ears. The gaiety dancing in Olivia's eyes grew stronger. She took a firm grip on Jasper's arm and glanced at him sideways.

"Would you promise me one thing?" she asked with a twinkle.

"What's that?" Jasper's pulse was already hammering. He was ready to lay his body down in front of steam trains or swim to the mainland all on his own, if only Olivia asked.

"Could you not take too long to purchase those two train tickets?"

The whole world dropped out of focus beyond Jasper's spectacles.

"You mean...you mean you'd come with me?"

"Of course I would."

Jasper all but tumbled out of the buggy seat.

"You mean you accept my proposal?"

"Yes!" Olivia cried joyfully. "Yes!"

As Jasper teetered in stunned astonishment, Olivia suddenly leaned over, grabbed him by the neck and began kissing him energetically. As Jasper struggled with the wonder of this, he completely forgot he was also driving a buggy. The reins jerked in his hands, the vehicle lurched sideways and the horse found itself standing up to its belly in wild asters and goldenrod. Jasper had inadvertently steered the entire outfit into the ditch!

The mishap only made Olivia laugh the louder, attracting the flabbergasted attention of Sara and Hetty, who had front-row seats on the veranda of Rose Cottage.

"I love you, Jasper Dale," Olivia declared, now knowing exactly the racing joy a woman should feel when she finally meets the right man to marry.

She began kissing Jasper all over again, even though Jasper was clinging to the last inch of the tilted buggy seat and would have fallen out altogether but for Olivia's grip. Jasper didn't know whether he was upside-down or right-side-up—only that Miss Olivia King was consenting to be his bride.

"Well," he gasped eloquently in the throes of romantic ecstasy, "ain't that the pistol, huh?"

On the veranda, Hetty King felt so completely topsy-turvy that she looked as though she might be speechless for a month of Sundays. As for Sara Stanley, she had no such difficulty. She was smiling from ear to ear, convinced, along with Peg Bowen, that, potions or no potions, magic really did happen in the world.